Falling for My Side Dude:

Renaissance Collection

Falling for
My Side Dude:

Renaissance Collection

Racquel Williams

www.urbanbooks.net

Urban Books, LLC
300 Farmingdale Road, NY-Route 109
Farmingdale, NY 11735

Falling for My Side Dude: Renaissance Collection
© 2017 Racquel Williams

ISBN 13: 978-1-62286-212-2
ISBN 10: 1-62286-212-0

First Mass Market Printing October 2019
First Trade Paperback Printing August 2017
Printed in the United States of America

10 9 8 7 6 5 4 3 2 1

Distributed by Kensington Publishing Corp.
Submit Orders to:
Customer Service
400 Hahn Road
Westminster, MD 21157-4627
Phone: 1-800-733-3000
Fax: 1-800-659-2436

ACKNOWLEDGMENTS

First and foremost, I give all praises to Allah. Without Him, none of this would be possible. I am forever grateful and definitely blessed.

To my mom, Rosa: thank you for being there through everything.

To Carlo: you know words can never explain how much you mean to me. I appreciate you.

To Nika, Ambria, Danielle, and Qiana: I appreciate the love and support I get from you ladies. I am forever grateful.

To Renee Fludd, and Sharlene Smith: thanks for the constant promotion of my work. I appreciate you ladies.

To my readers who have been rocking with me no matter what I'm going through, please know I appreciate y'all: Rhea Wilson, Yolanda Morgan, LaTanya Garry, Jeree Alyce, Patricia Charles, Barbara Morgan, Dawn Jackson, Cherri Johnson, Mary Bishop, Kendra Littleton, JoAnn Hunter-Scott, Toni Futrell, Priscilla

Acknowledgments

Murray, Joyce Dickerson, Nola Brooks, Erica Taylor, Yvonne Covington, Evelyn Johnson, Akia KiaBoo Porter, Latanya Burress, Jessica Deutaye Hudson, Dessiree Ellison, Donica James, Cherita Price, Redgirl Pettrie, Jane Pennella, Lisa Borders Muhammad, Alexis Goodwyn, Maya Gibson, Tonya Tinsley, Jocelynn Boffman Green, Taheerah Brown, Myre Childs, Sharon Bel, Aisha Taylor-Gamble, Pam Williams, Tammy Rosa, Shekie Johnson, Venus Murray, Shann Adams, Nancy Pyram, Tina Simmons, Patricia Charles, Temmiyyia Davidson, Nicki Williams Kenia Michelle, Jenise Brown, Kysha Small, Suprenia Hutchins, MzNicki Ervin, Trina McGuire, Rebecca Rogers, Rita King, Stephanie Wiley, Stacey Phifer Mills, Rochelle Simmons, Tera Kinsley-Colman, Joan Bro, Carol Mustipher, Charmain Trantham, and Kesia Ashworth-Lawrence.

To my readers out there, too many to name: thanks for rocking with me. If I forgot anyone, please charge it to my head and not my heart!

PROLOGUE

Paying bills, cooking, and helping out around the house are all things that most married bitches wished their husbands were doing, but not me. I may be coming off as ungrateful, but you'd have to take a walk in my shoes first in order to understand where I was coming from.

I met my husband, Trent, while I attended a party that an old friend was throwing at a banquet hall. He was this tall, dark-skinned brother with that look that made you scream, "Damn, who is that?" I guessed the feeling was mutual, because the entire night he kept on eyeing me. On his way out the door, he slipped me his number written on a piece of paper. After debating if I really wanted to call this man, I decided to take a chance. After talking, I realized that we had so much in common, and the best part of it was that he knew how to make me laugh. There was something about a man with a big sense of humor.

I learned that he was fifteen years older than me and, to be honest, at first it bothered me; but the more we conversed, the more I realized that his age wasn't a big factor to me. Plus, he treated me like a queen. We started dating, and soon we became inseparable. We dated for about two years, and then he proposed. I quickly accepted, and we had a big wedding, which was the talk of the town for years to come.

For the first years after we got married everything was great, or so I thought. Right after our wedding, I learned that I was pregnant; but it didn't last. Three months into my pregnancy, we learned that I miscarried. The loss of our child put a strain on our relationship a little, and Trent started staying out more.

I was tired of sitting at home alone doing nothing, so I decided to go to law school. I enrolled in the University of Richmond School of Law. In three years, I graduated with my law degree. This was something I dreamed of since I was young; I was fascinated with the Matlock and Perry Mason court shows.

Right when I was getting ready to start my career, Trent decided he was ready to retire. After all, he'd been a Richmond City Police homicide detective for over twenty years. I wasn't tripping that he didn't make a lot of money, because I had my own. My father passed away when I was only twelve, and he left a substantial amount of money behind. Let's just say that his children wouldn't ever have to worry about money. Mama was also well taken care of. She and my two older sisters moved from New York after I graduated high school and started college.

It was soon after college that Trent and I met. Right around our sixth anniversary, I noticed things started to change drastically. He would leave for days without calling or saying a word to me about where he was going or what he was doing. I also noticed that he had become distant and abusive. He'd try to start fights with me for no damn reason. He would threaten me, at times with his gun, and the words "bitch" and "slut" were his words of choice. It didn't take anything for those words to fly out of his mouth. At first, I kept praying for a change. I wanted my marriage to work out. I figured if I fucked him good and was a good wife, he would eventually change his ways. I was wrong; the more he got away with his bad behavior, the more he continued doing it.

To make matters worse, I found out I was pregnant with twins. I was excited because I was starting to think something was wrong with me because we had been trying to get pregnant right after the miscarriage. Trent, on the other hand, didn't seem too enthusiastic about the pregnancy. Once, he even mentioned that maybe I should get an abortion because he was too old to be a daddy. I was crushed when he said that because I thought he wanted a family; at least, that was what he had been screaming for years. I paid him no mind. I carried my children full term and gave birth to two bubbly baby girls.

Trent was present for their birth, even signed their birth certificate. I was hoping the birth of his daughters would soften him up a bit, but it didn't. In front of the girls and others, he was the doting, proud daddy; but behind closed doors he would curse me like a dog, accusing me of trapping him. I paid his ass no mind, and I put all of my attention into taking care of my girls.

I was ready for a change; I was tired of going through hell with this nigga. Matter of fact, I didn't want Trent anymore, so the first thing I did was start playing stingy with the pussy, and when we did have sex, I would lie there, pretending like the shit was good. I would throw it up on him, squeeze my pussy muscles, and talk dirty to him. In no time, he would bust. Trent just wasn't doing it for me anymore because of all the emotional ways he abused me; plus, he was a good size, but he just didn't know how to work the pussy. When I was younger, the dick was great, but the older I got, I realized that he wasn't as experienced as I thought. The only position he knew was him lying on top of me and stabbing me hard. He was boring, and whenever I suggested he try another position, he would curse me out bad and accuse me of fucking other guys.

I wasn't cheating, but I wanted something new! I wanted a man who could make my insides tingle, make my pussy wet just by looking at me, and fuck me for hours without busting. I wanted passion, the kind that made my toes curl and made my insides shiver.

See, I, Malaya Ipswich, was born and raised on the south side of Richmond, Virginia. I was raised in a home with both of my parents but, growing up, I could see that Mama wasn't happy; she just chose to settle. My daddy was a good man to everyone around him and a great provider, but he was not a good man to Mama. He had different women all over the city, and he paid them lots of money to keep quiet about the affairs. I wished Mama had a backbone to leave him, but she didn't. She played the good wife until we got word that he passed. As if that weren't bad enough, he had a heart attack while one of his mistresses was riding him during sex. I knew Mama was broken when she found out, but she quickly got over it after he was buried. I thought she was relieved to know he wouldn't be screwing around on her anymore.

I made a mental note back then: I wasn't gonna be like that. I wanted more out of a relationship. People may judge a bitch, may even go so far as to call a woman a bitch or slut if she was fucking another man. But did they really know what was going on in one's bedroom or in a relationship? Well, I can't speak for another bitch, but for me, if a nigga can't handle his business, whether it's in the bed or financially, he should be replaced. I'm not saying to divorce your husband or leave your man, but move his ass out of the way so that the next nigga can move on in and handle his business!

CHAPTER ONE

Malaya

I was irritated as hell as my damn alarm clock woke me up. I mean, I knew I had to be in the office but, shit, I wished I could get at least another hour. I reached over and cut the alarm off and threw the cover off of me. "Damn," I mumbled to myself as I sat up in the bed.

I instantly noticed that my husband was not on his side of the bed. My suspicions quickly kicked in, but I quickly dismissed the idea. I got up and grabbed my robe. I walked downstairs to make a cup of coffee. As soon as I stepped off the stairs, the smell of bacon filled the air. I walked into the kitchen and noticed that Trent was in there, cooking.

"There you are, you sleepyhead," Trent said as he flipped over the bacon.

"Ugggh, I think I had too much wine last night, and I have to be in the office. I have a new client coming in this morning."

"Well, you should hurry then. I already fixed breakfast. Here, get a cup of coffee." He placed the cup in front of me.

"Thanks. Lord, what would I do without you? You are a lifesaver," I said sarcastically.

"I'm the lucky one. Now, go on before you are late for your meeting." He smiled at me.

Without responding, I grabbed my cup of coffee and walked out of the kitchen.

To the public eyes, we were the perfect couple; but, in reality, this woman was far from being happy. I was a miserable woman, stuck in a fucked-up-ass relationship, with a man who wouldn't fucking leave.

I took a quick shower and ironed my suit. I didn't have time to really pamper myself, so I quickly oiled down and slipped into my two-piece Armani skirt suit. I then put on my Michael Kors heels that I just bought a few days ago. I sprayed a little bit of Dior J'adore perfume, took one last glance, and then grabbed my briefcase.

I was about to make my way down the stairs when I remembered that I didn't kiss the kids. My twelve-year-old twin girls were asleep in their bedrooms. I did a quick turn and went back up the stairs. I first went into Nyesha's room and kissed her on the cheek and then went to Myesha's room and did the same thing. My girls were definitely my life and the sole reason why I ground so hard. I made a vow when I was younger that when I did have kids, they wouldn't want for anything.

"Hey, I'm about to go. See you later," I said to Trent.

"Okay, I'll see you later. I have a luncheon to attend for one of my buddies."

"All right," I said as I stormed down the stairs and into the garage, where my 2014 BMW was parked. I got in and pulled out of our mini mansion in the Chesterfield section of Virginia.

I hated going into the city in the morning. Working in the city of Richmond definitely had its perks, but the traffic alone could cause a person not to accept positions anywhere downtown. Every morning was the same thing: bumper-to-bumper traffic all the way. I fully understood why some people parked their cars and carpooled together. I planned on doing that in the near future but, for now, I had to rough it out.

I parked in reserved parking and dashed out of the car. I practically ran into the building. I stood waiting for the elevator, hoping it would hurry the hell up.

I stepped out of the elevator and into my firm.

"Good morning, Mrs. Ipswich."

"Good morning, Dana."

Dana was my paralegal, and she was in law school, pursuing a law degree also. "Rough morning, I see," she joked.

"You have no idea. One of these days, I'm going to quit coming to the city. It doesn't make any sense at all how bad traffic is. Damn, this is Richmond; they need to figure out a way to fix this traffic problem fast."

"That's why I catch a ride every day with the van service. It saves me gas and the aggravation of dealing with these non-driving folks."

"See, you're the smart one," I joked before I walked into my office.

I threw my stuff on my desk and walked over to open my blinds. The beautiful Richmond skyline was lit up, and the midmorning sun was peeking in. I took a long sigh and then walked back to my desk. I was ready to tackle the world.

As soon as I sat down, Dana knocked at the door. "Come in," I yelled.

"I brought you some cappuccino; it will help to brighten your morning."

"Thank you, honey. Is Isiah here as of yet?"

Isiah was my law partner and good friend. I enjoyed working with him because he was young and hungry. I remembered the first time I witnessed him in action. He was like a young pit bull: fierce and determined.

"No, he's in court this morning. He won't be in until later this afternoon. So, it's just us."

"A'ight. I have an appointment at ten a.m. with Javon Sanders."

"Yes. His file is in front of you. I am about to go out front. Just buzz me if you need me."

"Thanks, Dana. What would I do without you?"

I took a sip of my cappuccino; this thing gave me life instantly. I picked up the folder in front of me and started to read up on a case. So, Mr. Sanders was charged with several felonies, which included distribution of cocaine and possession of a firearm by a convicted felon in the commission of selling drugs. Well, well, well. What do we have here? I continued reading the police account of what they said happened on February fourteenth when they burst up into the trap house where Mr. Sanders was at.

The ringing of the office phone interrupted my thoughts.

"Yes."

"Your ten a.m. appointment is here."

"Okay. Please direct him to my office." I got up and walked toward the door and opened it.

"Hello, Mr. Sanders. I'm Attorney Ipswich. Please step into my office."

"Hello," he said politely in a raspy voice.

"Please have a seat." I looked at the fine specimen of a man in front of me and couldn't help but wonder why he would choose a life of crime. "So, I believe my assistant discussed with you my fees if I decide to take your case."

"No disrespect, Mrs. Ipswich, money ain't a thing for me. You came highly recommended, so I definitely need you on the case." He smiled, showing his pearly white teeth.

"Is that right, Mr. Sanders?"

"Yup. Your name carries a lot of weight in the underground world. I know of a few cats who caught cases, and you got them off or got their charges reduced. So, I've got the money, and you've got the skills, so I think we can beat these charges that they tried to pin on me."

I could see that he had the same kind of mind frame as other criminals when they got arrested. They're never guilty, and the police are always framing them.

"Okay, well, I guess there's no need to argue with you. I will defend you, and you will pay me by cashier's check or money order, which you can give to my assistant on your way out."

"I got you! So, without sugarcoating shit, what are my chances of beating this case?" He stared me dead in the eyes.

He made my body shiver a little. He had these dark brown eyes that looked like he was piercing my soul. I could see that this nigga was trying to read me, so I looked down at the folder that was on my desk.

"Mr. Sanders, you're no stranger to the system, so you know the process. I will be contacting the DA's office in the morning to get a copy of their report. Then, I'll be able to get a better understanding of the route we need to take. You're out on bond, so you do know that you can't break the law. You catch a new case while this one is going on and, more than likely, your bond will be revoked, and you'll have to sit in jail until your case goes to trial."

"I got you." He flashed a smile.

"Here goes my card. You can call me anytime."

"Anytime?"

"You know what I mean. You can call me between business hours to discuss your case."

"What if I have an issue outside of business hours? Do I still call you?"

"Have a great day, Mr. Sanders." I got up and walked to the door.

He walked over to me, took my hand, and kissed it. "You're the sexiest lawyer I've ever seen, and I've seen many. I look forward to us working together."

"Likewise," I said.

I watched as he walked over to Dana. I closed my door and sat back down at my desk.

"Woeiii," I whispered.

Mr. Sanders was definitely a character. He was a little on the short side, but he was handsome with a strong voice. Whatever he was in, he was definitely on boss status. His in- control attitude made me feel some kind of way. I had to snap out of that fast. I was a law-abiding citizen, and he was a criminal. There was no way our paths could ever cross outside of business.

The rest of the day was spent on going over different cases that I was representing. I really loved my job as a defense attorney. I was known for my tenacity and no-nonsense attitude. I believed him when he said that my name was ringing bells in the streets because I was known for helping dope boys beat their convictions. Once in a while, I might lose a case, but even then my clients were happy with the reduced sentences that I got them.

My mind kept wandering back to Mr. Sanders. I'd never met a character like him. His case was a tough one, especially that gun charge, and I knew if I wanted to get him off I would have to put in extra work and use all of my skills.

It was past 4:00 p.m., and I was ready to call it a day. I tried not to take my work home, but today I made an exception. I grabbed Mr. Sanders's folder and my briefcase. I cut the lights out and walked out of the office. "You're ready?"

"Yes. I put the check in the safe. I will deposit it in the morning. I also responded to the e-mails and sent out all the e-mails."

"Thank you very much."

"You're welcome. I think that guy earlier has a crush on you," she said while smiling.

"Hmm. Why would you think that?"

"The way he looked at you. He also asked me if you were always this uptight. He smiled when he asked."

"Well, I didn't see that. Plus, I'm a happily married woman."

"I hear that loud and clear." She laughed.

We walked to the elevator, talking and laughing. We parted ways in the parking lot. I got into my car and pulled off. I wasn't ready to tackle this traffic. As bad it was in the mornings, the evenings were the same.

On the drive home, I couldn't help but think about my life. Here I was with a good job and a family who loved me, but I was not happy. I was tired of playing the happy wife while, inside, I was silently suffering. Yes, he played the doting husband and all but, to be honest, it was all a front. When no one was looking, Trent Ipswich was a cruel son of a bitch. As I recalled, something a year back had piqued my interest.

I was doing laundry, and I saw pink lipstick on his white collared shirt, which he supposedly wore to a retirement party for one of his boys. I put the shirt to my nose, and it smelled like sweat and cheap perfume. "Ewww." I quickly removed that shit from my nose and walked up the stairs. I walked into the study where he was and confronted his ass.

"So, who the fuck was lying up on you?" I threw the shirt on him.

"What in God's name are you talking about?" He looked at me like he had just seen a ghost.

"Pink lipstick on your shirt and that cheap-ass perfume! How do you explain that?" I stared down at him.

"Calm down. That is your lipstick, isn't it?"

"We've been married for how many years? You've never seen my black ass wear no damn lipstick. And I damn sure don't wear no cheap-ass perfume. Trent, you tried it, but please come up with something better than that," I snapped on that ass.

"I swear to you, Malaya, I'm not stepping out on you. I don't know where that lipstick came from. And as far as perfume being on my shirt, that's bullshit!"

I looked at this fool, sitting in front of me, sweating bullets; he was nervous as hell. I knew he was lying, and it only angered me that he thought he could feed me bullshit and I would believe him.

"I'm telling you this: you are a fucking fool if you think I believe a word that's coming out of your damn mouth. I'm not even mad. You're fucking one of your whores; at least now you can leave me the fuck alone."

I didn't wait for a response. I walked off on his ass and went back to doing what I was doing.

The honking of a horn jolted me back to reality. After that day, Trent started acting as if he was so in love with me again. I didn't say anything else about him cheating on me. That didn't mean that I didn't notice when his phone would ring late at night, and he would get up and tiptoe out of the room.

I'm not going to lie; at first, I was kind of hurt, or maybe I was more shocked. Up until that point, I really thought he was only a jerk, and he wasn't fucking anything. Even though I was angry with the way he treated me, I thought we could've gone to counseling and gotten our relationship back on track. But that day confirmed everything, and I gave up on hoping for a better us. I viewed him the same way that I viewed the rest of these fuck niggas who didn't know how to keep their dicks in their pants. Now, I couldn't stand his smell, much less his touch. Every time this bastard touched me, I cringed because I would rather he not touch me at all.

Things went from bad to worse. He became fascinated with fucking me in the ass all the time. Don't get me wrong, I can be a freak at times and, yes, I've been fucked in the ass before. However, I've got a pussy, which is tight and wet, so I didn't understand what my husband's sudden fascination with my asshole was all about. The first few times, I allowed him to grease up his dick and slide in. I also noticed that he would be more turned on when we were having anal sex than when he was up in my pussy.

"Trent, what's going on? Lately all you want to do is anal sex."

"Damn, Malaya! Why do you have to pick at every damn thing? Just toot your ass back here so I can get all the way in."

"You know what? Hell no. I ain't doing this shit no more. I'm a woman, and I've got a pussy. That's where I want to be fucked at."

I got up out of the bed and walked into the shower. That was the last time I allowed him to enter my ass and, because I refused to do it anymore, he stayed with an attitude. He barely asked for sex, which was cool by me. I bought a new We-vibe 4 vibrator, which satisfied me way better than Trent ever did. This was my first time using a toy and, boy, was I satisfied. I experienced multiple orgasms back to back, and my pussy was fully serviced.

I thought about getting a divorce but quickly decided against it. I wasn't going to leave my home and everything we'd accomplished so one of these whores could walk up in my shit and reap the benefits. I also wondered why he hadn't asked for one either, but I thought I knew the answer. He knew I would drag his ass through the mud and take my girls.

I slowly pulled into the driveway. I noticed Trent's car in the driveway, which was strange because he was supposed to be attending some sort of luncheon for one of his police buddies. I glanced at my watch; the girls were still at their afterschool band practice.

I got out of my car and walked toward my door. My palms were getting sweaty, and my throat started tightening up on me. I wasn't sure why he would lie to me about not being at home. I took my time and opened the front door. I slipped out of my loafers and tiptoed toward the stairs; something in me was yelling, don't go up there. I ignored the voice and quietly crept up the stairs. I heard screams, as in sexual screams, as soon as I approached my bedroom door. I walked to the door and slowly pushed the door ajar and stood there! Shocked would be an understatement. My husband, Trent, was fucking his slut in our marital bed that we shared.

"Fuck me, daddy! Fuck me, daddy," this slut screamed as he fucked her.

They were so into the heat of things that no one heard when I walked over to my dresser and took out my gun. I also pulled up my iPhone camera and started recording. I wanted to have proof of this nigga's antics.

"Hello, Trent!" I said.

"What the fuck? Uh-uh." He jumped off of her and turned around, looking at me with his dick still hard.

"Trent, who is this?"

"This is my . . ." he stuttered and acted like something was stuck in his throat.

"What's the matter, honey, the cat got your fucking tongue? Well, I'm his wife. Now, get the fuck up out of my shit before I blow both of y'all motherfucking heads off."

"Malaya, baby, I can explain. It's not what it seems. I can explain. Please put that gun down."

"Nigga, shut your motherfucking mouth. You're nasty as fuck. You bring this ho in my bed and, to make matters worse, your nasty ass ain't wearing no fucking condom. Now, get the fuck out!" I screamed and fired a shot in the wall.

"Are you fucking crazy? Put that thing down," Trent hollered.

The bitch scooted in the corner and crawled to retrieve her clothes. She gathered them and tried to run out the room. I was shocked as fuck! This wasn't a bitch. This was a nigga with a wig on his head. I just kept staring at this faggot standing in front of me with a dick the size of my arm. I swallowed hard and blinked a few times.

"Listen, you faggot, the next time you choose to fuck a married man, make sure he takes your ass to the hotel because you might end up dead over a dick that ain't yours in the first place," were the only words I managed to say.

"Bitch, fuck you. Trent is my dick; you better ask him." That cute little voice that I heard a few minutes ago was gone. This motherfucker was masculine as fuck. He looked at me and then stormed out the room, uttering some shit under his breath.

"Baby, please listen to me. I'm so, so, so—"

"Nigga, don't be sorry. You are a fucking faggot. You were in my bed, fucking another man! You nasty fuck, just get your shit and get out of my house. You will be hearing from my lawyer soon," I yelled with everything inside of me.

"Divorce? The one time I fucked up, you're screaming about divorce. I love you; I gave you every damn thing. Took you on expensive trips and made sure you never wanted for anything. You can't leave me," he said with confidence.

"See, I should just splatter your brain all over this fucking floor, but I ain't no dumb bitch. I've got too much shit going for myself to waste it on a garbage-ass nigga who is obviously a shit fucker. Oh, my God, no, how long have you been fucking dudes? Nah, don't answer that. Get your shit and get out before I do something I might regret."

"You're crazy as hell if you think I'm goin' to just walk away from my shit that I spent years building. This is my shit, you're my fucking wife, and those are my fucking kids. Y'all belong to me; you hear me? And you better delete that motherfucking video."

I pointed the gun at his dick. "What's the matter, Trent? You're worried that the world will see you in action? What do you think your mother will say when she sees her son pounding the next nigga's ass?"

"You bitch!" He lunged toward me.

"Get out or I'll shoot that ol' nasty-ass, limp dick off," I yelled as I took a step back.

He looked at me with his fist balled up. He shook his head and grabbed his clothes off the chair. "I'm leaving now because I don't feel like fighting with you but, best believe, I will be back."

I was going to say something but, instead, I just stared at this nigga. Actually, I felt bad for him because he had no idea what the fuck he was really saying. I was never a weak bitch, and I damn sure wasn't gonna start today. I watched as he grabbed a few things and stuffed them in a duffle bag. He mumbled something under his breath as he walked through the door. I really didn't care to know what he said. Seconds later, I heard the garage door go up. I walked over to my bedroom window, and I saw him backing out of the driveway.

I turned back around, and I stood there staring at the bed that they were just fucking in. I knew I had to get rid of the mattress. There was no way I was going to lie on that mattress that this faggot-ass nigga was fucking on.

I heard the door open, and I looked at my phone. It was time for the girls to come home. I walked down the stairs to make sure he wasn't coming back in.

"Hey, Mommy," they said in unison.

"Hey, my babies." I gave each of them a hug and a kiss on the cheeks. "Do y'all have homework?"

"I've got math and science," Nyesha said.

"I did mine on the bus," Myesha said.

"Okay, well, get to it, Nyesha; and tonight is a soup kind of night."

"All righty, Mother," they said as they walked off up the stairs.

I tried my best to not let on that anything was going on. My girls were very close to their daddy and, right now, I had no idea how I was going to break the news to them that their daddy was a faggot and that we wouldn't be a family ever again. I'd never lied to my children, and I wouldn't be starting anytime soon.

I walked into the kitchen and grabbed a bottle of red wine out of the cabinet and poured a tall glass. I was definitely hurt because, even though I suspected that he was fucking around on me, to actually see it in front of me kind of blew my mind.

I took a few big gulps and swallowed fast. I needed this. I wished I were a smoker because I definitely could've used a cigarette right now. "Damn you, Trent," I cried, and threw the glass into the wall. "Damn you. What a fool I've been," I said out loud.

I felt tears well up in my eyes, but I used everything in me to stop them. I refused to waste one tear on a nigga who had done me wrong. I walked off. I guessed I was sleeping in the guest bedroom tonight. I took a quick shower, made sure the girls were straight, and then I lay down until it was time to make dinner.

I tossed and turned all night. I couldn't believe the nerve of this man. I wondered how many other niggas I didn't know about he had brought up in my house. It sickened my stomach because I had sex with him, and I sucked his dick, the same dick that he stuck inside of another nigga's ass. I could have any kind of sexual disease and didn't know about it. Anger rose up in me as tears finally started to flow. I dug my face into my pillow and let it all out. I was hurting deep down, even though I tried to conceal it. I tried my damnedest, but I couldn't hold it in; my heart had a mind of its own. I cried until the tears were dried up. I thought about calling my mama, just to hear a few comforting words, but how would I tell my mama what I saw? I was too embarrassed to tell anyone. I lay there, thinking until I dozed off.

CHAPTER TWO

Malaya

I was up bright and early. I called the office to let Dana know that I would be working from home today. I had a few things to do like calling the locksmith so I could get these locks changed. I also needed to get Trent's shit out of my house. I knew the law, and I knew that I had to give him time to get his shit out, but I really didn't give two fucks about that.

I got dressed and got in my car. I needed to find a nice mattress, so I headed to Macy's; I thought that was where I bought my last one. On my way there, my mind was all over the place. I knew I loved my husband, but there was no way I could forgive him for what he did to me. I quickly dismissed that thought. I strongly believed that a man could only treat you the way you allowed him to treat you.

My phone kept ringing while I was driving, but I didn't bother to pick it up. I had a strong feeling that it was Trent. I really didn't have anything to say to that man. It was over for me.

I parked and got out of the car. I sashayed into the mall like I didn't have a care in this world. That was how great M·A·C makeup was, concealing pain.

I had to wait until tomorrow for them to deliver my mattress. As soon as I got home, I called the locksmith. Thirty minutes later, he arrived and changed all of the locks for me. I wouldn't feel safe in this house if Trent had a set of keys. I would hate if I had to kill my husband in front of his children.

I also called my doctor to set up an appointment to get checked out. I hadn't had any symptoms of any kind, but I had to be sure. Only God knew how long he'd been fucking other men.

"Oh, my God," I yelled out. Now it all made sense; this nigga was fucking me in the ass because he was a faggot. Not because my pussy was loose, but because that was what he loved to do. I racked my brain to see if there were any other signs, but there were none; he was married, he had children, and he was a macho dude.

He didn't have one feminine trait that I could think of. I was so confused. I even questioned what I saw, but I knew for a fact that the nigga Trent had in the room had a horse dick, almost touching his knees.

Even though I was sick to my stomach, I still had to cook dinner that night. My girls had soup the night before, so another night in a row was a no-no. I decided to bake some chicken thighs along with mashed potatoes and green beans. My appetite was gone, so I wasn't going to eat. However, I did pour me a glass of wine.

I sat at the table as the girls ate their dinner. I wanted to wait until another day, but I decided to get it over with now. "Girls, I need to talk to you, both of you."

"Did something happen, Ma? You're not dying, are you?" Nyesha joked.

"Ha-ha. No, not yet." I laughed at her. "Anyway, your daddy is not out of town like I said yesterday. The truth is, Daddy no longer lives here."

"What do you mean? He moved out?" Myesha quizzed.

"Well, your daddy did something bad to me, and I asked him to leave. Earlier today, I changed all the locks so he can't come back in here."

"Really, Mom? You're just goin' to throw Daddy out like that?"

"Listen, little girl, lower your damn voice before I do it for you. Like I said, your daddy did something bad, so he is not going to live with us anymore."

"I'm going to call my daddy. I know you're making this up." Myesha jumped up and ran out of the kitchen.

All I could do was put my head down. I knew how close my children were to their father, but Myesha was extra close with him.

"Don't worry, Mom. I understand." Nyesha walked over to me and hugged me.

I broke down crying in my child's arms. I didn't mean for this to happen. Maybe I should've let him stay, but how could I? He did the ultimate betrayal by bringing another nigga in my house. He violated our marriage and our home; there was no way around that.

After cleaning up, I decided to shower. As the water beat down on my skin, I let out every emotion that I was feeling. I bawled and bawled until I realized my body was numb from all the hot water that was beating down on me.

I turned the water off and got out. As I dried off, I couldn't help but imagine what it would feel like to have a man rub his hands across my perky breasts. Even though I had children, I was still able to maintain a cute, sexy figure. A sense of jealousy rushed over me as I flashed back to when my husband was deep into that nigga's ass. I hated his ass for not having the balls to walk away from me. Instead, he had to do this fucking shit. Everything was questionable now, from those long trips out of town to money missing from our joint account. Now it all made sense to me.

I tried to sleep, but I couldn't. I jumped out of the bed, ran downstairs, and grabbed a few trash bags and started taking all his clothes out of the closet and the drawers. I stuffed them in the bags, and I took all the expensive suits and leather shoes he owned and placed them inside the bags. I dragged them down the stairs, one by one, into the basement. Tears rolled down my face as I grabbed the big bottle of Clorox bleach and poured it all over his belongings. Making sure that even the socks were drenched with bleach, I tied the bags up and dragged them, one by one, out the garage door, out to the trash, by the curb. Pickup was tomorrow, so I needed to get this shit out of my house.

I walked back in the house, closed the garage, and walked up the stairs. I washed my hands and poured a glass of wine, grabbed a few crackers, and walked up the stairs. I dried my tears and cut the television on. I was trying to catch an episode of Wives with Knives. Now, I could see what these crazy bitches were going through when they went ham on those niggas.

CHAPTER THREE

Malaya

"Bye, Mommy, I love you," Nyesha said as she ran out of the house. I was expecting the same from her sister, but I saw she still had an attitude. God knows what lies her daddy told her when she called him. She walked past me without saying a word to me. I closed the door as the bus picked them up.

I didn't have any time to waste; I was having a meeting with Mr. Javon Sanders. Yes, you heard me right. Mr. Sanders, my client. For some reason, I was excited to see him today. This was strange because he was only a client. I had no right feeling like this. I quickly dismissed that thought.

In no time, I was dressed. I decide to wear my extra-tight pinstriped skirt suit. My hair was done, so I just spritzed some spray on it and made sure my edges were straight. I put a little lip gloss on my lips. After taking one last look at myself, feeling satisfied, I walked out of the room. I grabbed my briefcase and the pile of files I had.

I walked around the house, making sure all the doors and windows were locked. I didn't trust Trent. I hoped he'd just stay gone. Wishful thinking. He was a nigga who didn't believe in divorce, so I knew that, wherever he was at, he was plotting his next move. I knew one damn thing: somebody better tell that man to stay away from me before his mama be burying her only son.

I finally made it to work, on time. I parked my car and got out. I grabbed my briefcase and my papers and walked toward my office. Dana was off today. She had an emergency with her family back in Detroit, so she flew out there for a few days.

It looked like I was there by myself today. Oh, well, my client should be here in about another hour. I opened my blinds, made a cup of cappuccino, and turned my computer on. I had a little time to read e-mails and also respond to them. I turned on the video so I could know when he entered the office.

My phone started to ring. I grabbed it off my desk and answered. It was Trent.

"What the hell do you want?" I asked him.

"You know what I want. I just went to the house and realized that you changed the locks on me."

"It was your house, but you gave up that right when you were in my bed, fucking that nigga."

"That doesn't mean shit. You can't just put me out of my own shit. I fucking live here; I suggest you give me a key, or I'll call the police."

"I don't give a fuck about you calling the police. I would love to let them know what I caught you doing. You are not moving back in, so I suggest you find somewhere else to live. I will be divorcing you, and I will give them lawyers the video that I have of you screwing a transsexual in my bed."

I was done talking to his ass, so I hung the phone up. This bastard had some fucking nerve, calling talking about me changing the fucking locks. What the fuck did he expect? Did he think that we were going to lie in the same bed he was fucking that slut nigga in? See, my day was going fucking good until this nigga interrupted my day. I let out a long sigh and went back to what I was doing.

Twenty minutes later, I heard the office door open. I looked at the monitor and saw that it was Mr. Sanders walking in. My heart jumped a couple beats, and I had no idea why it did that. However, I straightened my skirt and walked out of the office and into the lobby.

"Hey there, Mr. Sanders. How are you?" I asked.

"Well, hello to the most beautiful woman I have ever laid eyes on," he joked and smiled.

"Come on back here. We have work to do." I walked off on him.

"Sure, I'll follow you wherever you want me to go."

I walked to the office, and he followed me. I took a seat behind my desk, and he sat in the chair in front of me. We started to discuss his case.

"So, you have a court date coming up in three weeks. I just want you to be ready for it. I've put in a motion for discovery, so I can see all of the evidence that they claim they have on you."

"So, how is it looking?" he asked.

"Well, you know I'm going to tell you the truth. According to their evidence, they have a lot of shit on you. But you know I'm good at what I do, so I've got a few tricks that I'm going to pull out to see if they work." I paused. "I need you to stay out of trouble; I need you to cut all these niggas loose. I need you to just stop running the streets, and I need you to get into a drug program."

"A drug program?" He looked at me, confused.

"Yes, a drug program. It will help you because it has a diversion program that you can go to instead of going to prison."

I wasn't going to lie; this nigga was looking good as hell in front of me. The way he licked his lips and his cocky demeanor were driving me crazy. My pussy lips started to tingle as I tried to move around a little bit in my chair without bringing attention to myself. I didn't know what it was about this man, but I swear I wished that I was bouncing up and down on his dick right now. I knew I was tripping, but I was horny as fuck, and we're both grown, so we could definitely do what grown people do: get our fuck on.

"Mrs. Ipswich, you okay?" His voice interrupted my thoughts.

"Uh-huh. Yeah, I'm good. I just got sidetracked for a second."

"Oh, okay, 'cause you were looking kind of crazy." He burst out laughing,

I giggled a little, but I was embarrassed. Here I was, in the company of a hot-ass street nigga, and I was fumbling over my words. I hurried up and regained my composure.

"Okay, back to what I was saying. I need to know if you'd be interested in taking a plea deal if they offer one."

"A plea deal? What do I look like? A fucking rat, B? I mean, I'm a real G. I ain't wit' no snitching shit," he yelled.

"You need to stop yelling and talk. Get out of your hood mentality for a quick second. I wasn't saying anything about no snitching. But, shit, what I heard was that some of your so-called friends were trying to plead out. I suggest you think about you and you only. There are no friends in these streets. I've been in this business long enough to see husbands roll over on wives and vice versa, mamas telling on sons and vice versa. Those same niggas who you are faithfully riding for will be the niggas copping pleas so they can get less prison time," I spat at him.

It disturbed the fuck out of me to see these so-called street niggas run around here talking about, "Loyalty over anything." Really? While the niggas they were loyal to were setting them up?

"Damn, you got a little harsh, didn't you?"

"Harsh? No. I'm giving it to you straight. You're a street nigga, so you should want it straight. I'm a damn great lawyer, but it irritates me when my clients be acting like they have no idea how serious their charges are."

"Trust me, I get it. But you need to get it; I live and breathe these streets. You see this?" This arrogant-ass nigga unbuttoned his shirt, pulled his wife beater up, and revealed his tattoo that went across his chest: LOYALTY OVER EVERYTHING. "I live this. I will lay it down for life before I roll on any one of my niggas. I don't know what the next man is doing; I'm only responsible for what Javon does. You feel me?"

"Understood, Mr. Sanders."

We ended up discussing his case a little bit longer. Then, he was ready to go. I got up, about to walk him out. He stood by the door.

"Excuse me," I said as I tried to pass him.

"Why are you fighting it?"

"Fighting what?" I laughed nervously.

"Come on. From the first day we met, I knew I was digging you, and today, you confirmed that you're feeling the same way. So, we're grown. Why are we playing these little children games? I have no idea."

"Mr. Sanders, I have no idea what you're talking about! I'm your lawyer; you're my client. Nothing more, nothing less." I smiled at him but, deep inside, I was exploding. I wanted to feel his big hands rubbing across my chest. I wanted to feel his lips pressed against mine.

"Let's see if I'm tripping." He took a step and pulled me closer to him, locking his big lips down on mine.

"What are you doing?" I managed to mumble between kisses.

"Doing what we both want," he said as he started fondling my breasts through the silk blouse that I had on underneath my suit. I tried to move, but my mind was stuck, and I couldn't allow myself to move. I started kissing him back as I inhaled his masculine smell. He unbuttoned my shirt and released my breasts from my bra. I started to unbutton his pants. I felt his dick; it was already hard. It wasn't an average-size dick; baby was packing in the right places. My pussy was going through all sorts of different emotions. I was yearning for a dick to make my hungry pussy satisfied. Before you knew it, we were both butt-ass naked in my office.

He lifted me up without warning and placed me on top of my office table, pushing all my papers over. He threw my legs over his shoulder, while he knelt down on his knees and slowly inhaled the fresh scent of my neatly shaved pussy. Feeling his breath on my clit kind of made me edgy. He then licked the tip of my clit, causing me to tremble inside. Before I knew it, he was head deep into my opening. I wrapped my legs and locked his head deep in. I lay down with my eyes closed. I blocked everything out of my mind; I was trying to savor the moment.

"Awee, aweee," I screamed out when he sucked aggressively on my clit.

I definitely loved every moment of this. I wasn't big on dick but getting my pussy sucked was another thing. I rose up a little bit and held on to his shoulders as I came all in his mouth. I tightened my grip as I climaxed a few more times. He got up, and without notice, he flipped my ass around like I was a rag doll. He slid his dick all up in my wet pussy.

"Hmmm," I mumbled.

I assumed it was a good size; I didn't know it was that big. So, I was definitely under the pressure; the farther he slid up in me, the more pressure I was under. The pain was bad, but the dick was everything. I loved it. I knew that sounded crazy, but it was good and bad at the same damn time. I tried to move around, but he had me pinned down, and he wasted no time beating my walls down. The hard-ass table didn't help anything. I closed my ass and took that dick like a grown woman. I didn't know the time, but I assumed it was twenty minutes later. I felt like he was thrusting harder, so I used everything in me to throw my ass back on him. His dick got stiffer, and within seconds, he busted.

"Arrghhhhh. Fuck! Fuck," he growled out.

I quickly turned around and jumped off the table. Even though I enjoyed it, I was happy it was over with because that table was hurting my stomach, and the pressure he was applying from behind wasn't helping either. He stood there in front of me with his dick hanging, and he looked at me. "Yo, you got that good, good."

I looked at him. I wasn't sure how I should respond. "I can't believe I did this. This is so not me," I said.

"Relax, yo! You're grown, and you looked like you could've used a good fuck."

"Excuse me? What are you saying? I looked thirsty?"

"Nah, I mean you seem uptight, like it's been a minute since you had your pussy beat up."

"I'm a married woman, and I am not backed up," I lashed out.

"Chill out. You're getting all defensive and shit. Ain't nothing wrong if ol' boy don't know how to satisfy a woman of your caliber."

I didn't say anything. I picked my clothes up off the carpet. I was kind of embarrassed that I allowed this to happen, especially because he was my client. Furthermore, his ass was arrogant as hell.

I was happy no one else was in the office that day because I would've been embarrassed as hell. I walked in the small bathroom in my office and grabbed lots of paper towels, and I wet them. I washed between my legs as much as I could and then got dressed. My hair was all over the place, so I used my fingers to straighten it out a little bit.

I mustered up the nerves to walk back into my office. He was already dressed and sitting down. I was hoping that he would've been gone, but I saw that he had other plans.

"You're still here?" I asked.

"Hell, yeah. Where did you think I was going, especially after this good fuck you just gave me?"

"Well, you're from the streets, like you said, so here it goes. This was a one-hit acquittal. 'No strings attached' fuck. Forget it ever happened because I'm a married woman, and you're a thug."

"Damn, that's cold, but I ain't got no plans to leave you alone. I'm feeling you. You're a bad bitch in court, and you've got some good pussy."

"First off, I'm a grown woman, not a bad bitch! Just because I fucked you doesn't mean you know me. I saw a nigga with good dick, and I was horny, so we fucked. Unless it has to do with your case, please don't contact me. Now, can you please leave so I can get some work done?"

"A'ight, you got that, ma. But you've got my digits; hit me up."

He winked at me, opened the door, and walked out. I looked at the monitor as he walked out of the office. After the door closed behind him, I got up and walked into the waiting area and locked the office. I walked back into my office and flopped down on my sofa. I sighed. I couldn't believe I just fucked him and ran him off. That seemed like a ho move, but after the way this man fucked my soul, mind, and body, I couldn't stand to be in his presence.

The rest of the day was spent trying to work, but I barely got any work done. My mind was stuck on this thug. I wondered what it would feel like to be with him, not sexually, but in a relationship. I knew a nigga like him, with all that money and good dick, definitely had a bitch, or a few of them to be exact.

It was a bit early, but I decided to call it a day and leave. I was smelling like pure sex; there was no way I could handle any kind of business smelling like dick and pussy mixed together. I cut the computer off, grabbed my things, and left.

This was one of those days when I wished I lived closer. I was tired from cumming so much and just wanted to shower and get in bed.

CHAPTER FOUR

Malaya

Talk about being dick whipped! Ever since that boy dicked me down in my office, I couldn't seem to get him out of my mind. I was kind of confused because I wasn't looking for a man, especially after what I'd just gone through with Trent. But the way he fucked me good made it hard for me to forget about him. It was strange that he was feeling the same way. Most days after work, we would get together at the Marriot hotel on Broad Street. It wasn't a cheap hotel, but it was very private. I couldn't risk being seen by any one of my peers. That would definitely be the talk of the town, and I wasn't ready to be the center of everybody's attention. This dude never failed to amaze me; each visit turned into something great. Room service was on point and, after we ate, he would fuck me so good my pussy would hurt for days.

He woke up something inside of me that I thought was gone for good. For years, I couldn't get wet for Trent, and I thought there was something wrong with me. Now I knew that there wasn't shit wrong with me. My pussy stayed wet all the time. If Javon ran across my mind, my pussy started to moisten, and when he was close by, I could feel my drawers soaked with pussy juice.

Whenever there is happiness, there's always bullshit following close by. I got home from work a little later one night. I fixed the girls' dinner, and I was about to take a quick shower so I could meet up with Javon. Lo and behold, as soon as I stripped my clothes off, I heard a loud-ass banging on the door. It was strange because whoever it was wasn't ringing the bell; they were banging on the door.

"Damn," I blurted out as I hurriedly wrapped my robe around my body. I walked down the stairs with an attitude. "Who is it?" I yelled in a high-pitched tone.

"Chesterfield police, ma'am."

The police? What the fuck are the police doing here? I peeped through the peephole, and I saw two police officers.

"Officers, how may I help you . . ." I didn't finish my sentence because I instantly spotted my husband standing with them.

"Ma'am, Mr. Ipswich called us to accompany him. He informed us that he lives here, but he has been unable to enter the residence because you've changed the locks."

"Did Mr. Ipswich also tell y'all that he got caught fucking another man in our bed?" I stared him down.

"Malaya, they don't need to be involved in our personal business. I just want to come back home."

"You dumb-ass nigga, you brought them into our business. I told your ass I don't want you here." I was fuming with anger.

"Ma'am, calm down. According to the law, you can't just put him out. You have to go through the courts and properly evict him. If not, it's an illegal eviction, and you can be forced to pay him a substantial amount of money."

"I know the law; I'm an attorney. I swear, I can't live with this man. You all are making a mistake," I pleaded.

"Do you have somewhere you can go then, ma'am?"

"Hell no. This is my shit; I ain't going nowhere. So him and his slut can come up in my shit? I work too damn hard to just walk away."

I saw that I wasn't getting anywhere with these people, so I hissed through my teeth, turned around, and walked into my house. I was fucking mad; I didn't want this nigga here. I swear I didn't.

"Daddy is home. Daddy, I miss you so much," I heard Myesha yell out to him.

God, I can't do this. I refuse to live like this.

"Where the fuck are you going?" I asked as he walked into my room.

"What do you mean? This is my room too."

"Not no fucking more! You won this battle, but I promise I will drag your ass into divorce court. I will make sure you feel every bit of my wrath."

"You know what, Malaya? You are one miserable bitch. If you want a reason why I fuck these niggas and bitches, take a look in the mirror. You are one miserable bitch, always complaining. You acted like my dick was garbage; well, guess what? These boys love fucking and sucking me off, and their asses are way tighter than that sloppy pussy you have between your legs. He wasn't the first one; he's just the only one you know about. Now let that sink in, bitch," he said as he turned around and walked out.

This was the first time I was actually at a loss for words. My brain tried to comprehend this, but I couldn't. I stood there, frozen, as this man told me how he really felt. Normally, I would have had a comeback. After all, I'm an attorney; but this time around, I wasn't in the courthouse.

This was my life, my showdown, and I couldn't come up with an argument. It took me a few minutes to move out of the spot I was in. I got up and slammed my door. I just sat there, staring at the ceiling.

The ringing of my phone interrupted my thoughts. I reluctantly answered the phone. "Hello."

"Hey, love. Are you ready?"

"No, I'm not going anywhere," I said, a little harsher than I intended.

"Damn, B, you good? You sound like you're pissed off or something."

"No, I'm not feeling good. I'm just going to stay in tonight."

"A'ight, that's cool. Hit me later if you want."

I hung up the phone, feeling like shit. He was the only hint of happiness I had, and here I was, snapping on him. I didn't mean to bring him into my drama-filled world. I locked my room door, and then I threw the phone on the dresser. I grabbed my gun and lay across my bed. Is this what my life has come down to? I held my gun in my hand. I was prepared to shoot if this nigga even breathed on me.

I decided to take the day off. I didn't have to be in court today; plus, Dana was back from visiting with her family.

Javon and I decided to meet up for lunch. The motion for discovery came back on Javon's case. It was more than I expected. They had him on several recordings setting up big drug deals. They also had an informant talking about how he and his crew murdered other rival drug dealers. I let out a long sigh. This was way more than I bargained for. The man I admired so much was so far from the man the state was accusing of doing these gruesome things. I wished I would've looked deeper but would that have stopped me? No. I wasn't going to make any kinds of excuses. I wanted him since the first day I laid eyes on him. I wasn't in love with him or anything like that, but I enjoyed his company, and the dick was the bomb. At times, I imagined us being together in a relationship, but I quickly caught myself. There was no possible way we could have a long-term relationship, at least not right now.

We decided to meet up for lunch at Red Lobster. After what I learned earlier, I really didn't have much of an appetite. I got there earlier than him, so I parked and walked inside. I tried to switch my mood up a little, but I knew how serious things were.

"Hey, babe," he greeted me and kissed my lips.

"Hey, you." We both walked up to the hostess desk.

"Hello, how many?"

"Just two."

"Okay, follow me."

That was a first. I guessed it was because it was early in the day because Red Lobster is known to be slow.

She sat us all the way in the back, which was fine because what I was about to discuss with him was very private.

"What's going on with you, beautiful? You want to tell me why you were bugging last night?"

I thought of lying to him but quickly changed my mind. It was time for me to come clean with him. "Well, you do know I'm married, right?"

"Yeah, so?"

"When we first started talking, we were separated, but now, he is back in the house. He made me angry last night. That's all."

"So, you're still fucking him?"

"No, that's not what I'm saying. All I'm saying is he is back at the house, and now we are in separate bedrooms."

"Oh, okay. Why is that nigga even a factor in this?"

"He is not a factor. I was only telling you what was going on last night."

We ordered our food, and after we ate, I dropped the bomb on him. He was visibly upset by the news I just gave him.

"Listen, babe, you're gonna have to give me something to fight them with."

"Man, I'm fucked up right now. I don't know what to fucking do. Man, doing a bid ain't in my motherfucking plans."

I reached across the table and grabbed his hand. "Babe, I want you to trust me. I will do everything in me to fight this case. We are gonna fight this. You hear me?"

He didn't respond. I couldn't imagine what he was going through right now. I knew one thing: when you were in the streets like he was, it wasn't easy when you got caught up.

Lunch was basically over after we discussed his case. His whole demeanor changed. I tried to do little chitchat here and there, but anyone could see that he wasn't feeling any of that shit.

"Yo, how long do you plan on staying at the same house as your husband? I mean, eventually he's gon' want to fuck," he said with an attitude.

"Are you serious right now? I mean, all we've been doing is fucking and sucking. Not one time did you come out and say anything about your intentions with me. Plus, you have a serious-ass case going on."

"What the hell does that have to do with anything? You're talking like you know for sure that a nigga goin' to do time," he yelled.

"You need to lower your fucking voice. I'm a lawyer and a damn good one. Your case is a hard one. They've got your dumb ass on tape arranging drugs deal and setting up murders and shit. I'm your only fucking hope right now."

"You need to chill out. I 'ont need no-damn-body but, God, don't get in your feelings 'cause I ask you 'bout ol' boy. Shit, I wanna know what your plans are. Am I just the side nigga or what? 'Cause I ain't got no problem with beating your back out, but all this spending money, eating out, and extra shit, I ain't with it."

"Sometimes you need to keep your damn mouth shut because the more you open it up, the more stupid you sound. As far as my husband and me, we are separated, and that's that! When you make me your woman, then I will answer to you. Now, you please have a good fucking day. Call me when you're ready to be more than my side nigga."

Without saying anything else, I threw the fork on the plate, along with the napkin. Grabbing my purse, I stormed out, leaving him sitting there alone. I noticed the people sitting on the side looking at me like they were listening to our conversation all along. I shot them a dirty look and continued walking out. I wasn't in the damn mood. This nigga just took me there; I wasn't one of those old ghetto-ass bitches who be acting out in public. I was a professional woman, and I preferred to remain just that.

I jumped in my car and sped off. I was definitely in my feelings. I was mad at myself because I let him take me there. In a way, I felt where he was coming from, but I didn't have the answers about Trent. I wanted a divorce, but I didn't want to file for a divorce. God, I wished that bastard would have a stroke or something; that way I could bury his ass and still have my money left. See, Trent had money, but the majority of the money came from my wealthy dad who died and left me a hefty inheritance. My ass was young, dumb, and full of cum, so I didn't let him sign a prenup, so here we were now. This cheating-ass bastard could walk away with a good portion of my money. See, I wanted to explain this to Javon, but the last thing I needed this street nigga knowing was that I was a wealthy woman. Can't trust even the nigga you're sleeping with. I was also annoyed that he was pressing me about my relationship status with Trent. I mean, he was only the nigga I was fucking. He didn't have all those damn rights.

Call me paranoid, but after I left Red Lobster, I noticed a dark-colored car following close behind me. I brushed it off, but the car kept on my ass. I turned on a different street, and the car still followed me. I was nervous because I had no idea who might be following me. I decided to drive to the nearest police station, which was about two blocks from where I was. I sped down the road, hoping the car would turn off somewhere else.

My palms were sweaty, and my heart was racing. I pressed the gas a little harder. I was happy as hell when I saw the police station. I turned inside and parked. The car stopped, waited a few seconds, and then pulled off. I thought about going in the station, but I really didn't know what to say, and I wasn't sure who it was in that car. After waiting a few minutes and not seeing the car, I decided it was safe to pull out. I kept glancing in my rearview but saw no sign of the car.

When I got on my block, I circled it twice before I pulled into my driveway. I was still troubled because I wasn't sure who was in the car and why they were following me. I quickly jumped out and stormed into the house. I locked the door and peeped through the window. I didn't see a sign of another car. I closed the blinds and walked into the kitchen.

Javon

Mom-Dukes named me Javon, but the hood knew me as Young Killa because that's exactly what I was. Ever since I was young, growing up on Chimborazo Boulevard in Richmond, I knew I was about that life. The life of robbing and selling drugs, that is. I committed my first murder at the age of fifteen. Funny thing was, I didn't feel no way when I killed that nigga. Instead, I felt powerful. It was at that tender age that I earned my stripes among the old heads.

At twenty-six years old, ain't shit changed. My crew and me were causing havoc all over the streets of Richmond and Henrico County. We controlled mostly every block over on Chamberlain Avenue. Niggas either joined us or felt the wrath of our guns. We were street niggas, and in the streets, respect was earned, not given.

I had a crew of four hardcore killers. Mann-Mann was my right hand. I could trust that nigga with my life, and he could do the same with me. The other three niggas were Sword Man, Li'l Trigger, and my nigga, D. Drizzle. I grew up with these niggas, and I trusted them to a certain extent. So far, they'd proven nothing but loyalty to a nigga.

I thought shit was good; that was, until the task force burst up in the trap. I was sick as fuck 'cause all the work and the money were up in here since it was early as fuck. It kind of shocked me, though, because we had just moved to this location, and only the four of us

knew about this location. I didn't think anything at first.

On the way down to the lockup, D. Drizzle
kept trying to talk about business and shit.

"Yo, shut the fuck up. You know where we at,
right?" I asked with an attitude.

"My bad, my nigga."

The rest of the niggas looked at me like I was
out of pocket, but I wasn't. Niggas' mouths be
having diarrhea and now wasn't the fucking
time. I was extra tight 'cause they'd got all my
damn money. Earlier, I counted over thirty
stacks. Shit, a nigga was hurting bad.

I was given a bond. Mann-Mann and D. Drizzle
also got bonds. My two other niggas had warrants
in Chesterfield for a previous case and were
denied bond.

After I got bonded out, I went to go see my
old head, Abraham. That wasn't his real name,
but he earned that name 'cause he was like the
godfather of the underground world. I parked
in the lot and walked through the back of the
building. I banged on the door.

"Who dat?"

"It's me. Young Killa."

The door popped open, and I stepped in. I
knew he was standing behind the door with a
choppa. I'd been coming here for years, so I

knew the routine. "It's only me, Godfather. You can put the choppa down." I laughed.

"You already know how it goes, young'un." He stepped out from behind the door.

"What's good, fam?" I gave him dap and a quick hug.

"Nothing, shit. I hope you circled the block before you brought yo' hot ass up in here."

I was a little irritated by the way he was coming off, but I knew he had to be this way because the feds had been trying to get at him for years. They could never pin anything on him because he moved so smooth. "You already know I'm on point."

"What is all this I'm hearing about the pigs running up in your shit the other day?"

"Yup, they ran up in there and got the work and some paper. Shit crazy, yo."

"Yo, you hardheaded. There's no reason your ass should've been up in there. That's what you have workers for. Why do you think they could never link me to anything? Because I don't mingle in that shit. I just sit back and collect my money. I 'ont talk on no phone, none of that shit."

"Man, they got me on a bunch of charges. Shit don't look too good, yo."

"You will learn. I been told you that I heard rumors that one of them niggas in your camp was a fucking rat. I done told yo' ass don't bring them niggas round here."

I just sat there taking in what he was saying. Old Head knew some shit because he done seen it all. I just didn't believe that I had a rat in my camp. Ain't no way none of my niggas were working with the police. Hell nah, I was not even goin' to entertain that bullshit. We ended up chopping it up for a little, and then I bounced.

"I'm about to bounce. Just needed to kick it wit' you for a little bit."

"Javon, don't let your loyalty to these niggas cloud your judgment. Everybody is suspect when it comes down to the streets; even your mama can't be trusted. You need to check this lawyer out; she is a bad-ass bitch in the court-room. You goin' to need her." He grabbed my arm and handed me a card.

"I got you," I said as I opened the door and walked out into the brisk Virginia wind.

As I walked to my car, I had an uneasy feeling. I'd known Abraham since I was a young'un, and I trusted him, but sometimes I felt like the nigga was paranoid. I looked down at the card he handed me. It had a lawyer's name and number on it. I opened my car and got in. As I sat there, warming up the car, all kinds of thoughts were going through my head. I reached in my armrest and pulled out a blunt that I was smoking off earlier. I lit that shit and pulled off.

From the first time I laid my eyes on that bitch, I knew she was a freak. The way she looked at me, I knew I was going to bang that ass one day! I heard she was a beast in the courtroom, so if this bitch was as good as everybody said, I definitely needed her on my team.

I noticed the way she looked at me the first day we met. I was about my business, though; I needed this bitch to help me beat these charges. Don't get me wrong; I had no problem tearing that pussy up along the way! I knew one thing about bitches: if you fucked them right, they would fight for you to the very end.

I didn't think it was going to be easy, but being the nigga I was, I had to try my hand. From the minute I walked into the office and saw that the secretary wasn't there, I knew I had a chance to tear that ass up. I gave this bitch the dick, and I knew she was going to be hooked. I hate to sound conceited, but a nigga's paper was long, and I've got that big dick that curves at the tip. I ain't met a bitch yet who didn't like this pipe.

I had my girl, Tania, and I wasn't trying to wife no other bitch. She was my everything, even though I be fucking around. She was the mother of my daughter and my little man, and I swear, I did love that chick. She was there for a nigga when I ain't had shit. I remembered when we used to stay in the projects over in Jackson Ward. My baby's mama used to sell her food stamps to make sure I could get money to cop a pound of weed. That's when I knew I had to make it so she and my seeds would be straight.

After I had my first good lick, I moved them out of the hood and into a house on Broad Rock Boulevard, over on the south side. Even though I was doing my fuckery in the streets, I still made sure she knew she was my everything and that a nigga wasn't shit without her.

After ol' girl and I started talking, I had to juggle being with her and still being able to make my baby mama feel like she was still my main squeeze. I couldn't risk her finding out about this. She done had plenty of run-ins with bitches I done smashed. I hoped it didn't come to it this time because I needed this lawyer bitch to help me beat this case. I figured that if I acted like I wanted her and let her think that we were in a relationship, she would do everything in her power to keep me out of prison. I heard she was friends with a few judges. Shit, she might need to run that pussy to help a nigga out.

CHAPTER FIVE

Malaya

Javon and I became inseparable. Every chance we got, we spent time together. Days turned into weeks and then months. It's funny how time flies when you're having fun. I was no longer worried about my marriage or even the bitches or niggas Trent was fucking. I tried my best to focus on my work and getting my pussy satisfied. At times, I had to check myself because Javon made it so easy to fall for him.

It was hard at times because I would walk through the door and there was Trent, sitting in the living room. I would shoot him a look and then run upstairs to my room. Most times, I was tired of fucking and didn't have a bit of energy left in me to fight with Trent. Living with him was hell. Even though he barely said anything, I could feel him watching me at times. It was scarier than anything. There was something about his stares that gave me an eerie feeling.

I had court all day today, and I lost this one case that I thought I was going to win. This one weighed heavily on me because my client was a woman who shot a man who had been raping her small daughter. These fucking jurors came back with guilty for manslaughter. Shit, if I was in the same position, I would've killed that bastard also.

I poured a glass of wine and took a bite out of the hot wings that I bought. I wished I could get out of this funk. It's crazy how people who are actually innocent can end up getting time, and people who are guilty get to walk. I really loved what I did, but cases such as this one made me question my career choice.

The weekend was here, and I took the girls over to Trent's mother's house. I wished my mother lived closer so they could visit her the way they visited his mother.

I made it back to the house. I noticed Trent's car was parked on the side. I swear, I wished this man would just get the fucking picture and move out. I opened the door and walked in. I stepped on the stairs but turned around at the sound of his voice.

" Oh, yeah, bitch, I realized the other day my clothes were gone. Where are my fucking clothes at, bitch? My fucking closet is empty. You better have a good fucking reason," he yelled, waving his gun around in the air.

"I threw all of them out. Shit, most of the clothes you owned were bought with my money. When I met your ass, all you had was a few pairs of jeans and two suits. You didn't even own a fucking decent pair of drawers."

"Did you give my clothes to your man?"

"What the hell are you talking about? Just because you are a whore doesn't mean I'm going to be one."

"I see everything. I've watched you as you've come home from work, showered, got dressed, and left. I hear you coming in the house at all times of the night. I ain't no fool, Malaya. I know one thing; I won't be disgraced around town by some young punk because my wife wants to be a whore."

He caught me off guard with that one. What would make him think I was fooling around? Was he following me or paying someone to follow me? I swallowed hard to calm myself down. I couldn't let him see me sweat.

"Well, Trent, let me tell you this. This is my pussy, and I can fuck whoever the fuck I want to fuck. Just because we're married on paper doesn't mean you own me. I am done with you, so you better leave me the fuck alone. You're gonna get high blood pressure worrying about who I'm fucking with."

Slap! Slap! Slap! "Bitch, I will kill you! Trust me, you have no idea who you're fucking with." He stood over me, yelling.

I grabbed my face as this bum attacked me, slapping me in the face. I fell into the wall. I didn't stay down. I picked myself up and ran up the stairs and opened the drawer, but my gun was gone.

"Are you looking for this?" He stood there, smiling, with my gun in his other hand.

My heart dropped when I realized I had no way to protect myself. He looked like he had been drinking, and his eyes were glossy. I had no idea what was going through his head. I tried to map out an escape plan.

"You're not so powerful now, Miss Lawyer! I done told your ass, I ain't going anywhere. Better yet, I will leave you the fuck alone if you sign over one of these vacation properties to me, put $350,000 in my account, and also pay spousal support and child support since you're going to allow the kids to live with me. My children will never be around their slut-ass mother and her convict boyfriend. Only then will I leave you the fuck alone." He lunged toward me and started choking me.

I tried scratching his face, but he squeezed harder. I tried to breathe, but I barely could.

"Bitch, I could finish you off right now, clean this shit up, and bury your ass without anyone knowing. All I've got to say is that you ran off with that thug you're fucking! Now, think about the proposition I made or deal with it. We will be married until death do we part." He squeezed harder and then let go. He shoved me hard, and I fell on the carpet.

I started coughing as tears flowed from my eyes while I felt my neck. "You should've killed me because you will regret this. I promise you, Trent Ipswich," I managed to say in between coughs.

"Bitch, shut up! I was a good fucking man. All I did was fuck a slut in our bed, and you went off. You're one ungrateful bitch. At least I didn't have no outside kids or bring you home any damn diseases."

I managed to get myself up off the ground. I stood up with tears rolling down my face. "Ha-ha. You want a fucking trophy for that? If you weren't so busy fucking other niggas, I wouldn't have to fuck anybody else. You ain't no better than these woman beaters out here. I'm done talking to your ass, but please know I will pay you the fuck back for having the balls to put your hands on me."

"Yeah, yeah. Don't forget I've got friends in the precinct, and yes, I will be holding on to this." He shook my gun in the air. He then walked out of my room.

I sat down on my bed and massaged my neck. The physical pain was bad, but my mental state was far worse. I couldn't believe that he just did that to me. I wasn't no weak bitch, so how did I just sit there and let this nigga put his hands on me like that? "Noooooooo," I screamed out with everything in me, letting out all the frustration that I was feeling.

I got up, closed my door, and then I ran to my bathroom. I checked my neck, and it was bright red, compared to my olive skin complexion. I took two Aleve, and then I went on a mission. When I was finished, I ran in my room, crying, and grabbed my phone. I dialed Javon's number.

"Please pick up," I said to myself.

"Hey, love. I was waiting to hear from you."

"Hey. He found out 'bout me and you. Can you meet me please?" I cried like I was dying.

"What the fuck? Yo, meet me now on Broad Street and Cary Street by the carwash. I'll be there," he yelled into the phone.

I didn't say anything. Instead, I hung the phone up. Grabbing my purse, I opened my door and peeped out to see if he was in the hallway.

The coast was clear, so I ran down the stairs, into the garage. I jumped in my car and pulled off. Blood was dripping from my face, so I used a towel I had to soak up the blood. I drove like a crazy woman, but I still kept looking behind me. I had a feeling that the car I saw earlier was Trent or one of his cronies. I cried the entire way there. I pulled up at the carwash that he told me he was at. When I spotted his car, I pulled in beside him. As soon as I saw him approaching the car, I turned up the volume of my cries.

He knocked on my window. I let it down, giving him the shock of his life. "What the fuck is wrong with your face?" he yelled.

I started crying harder. He went around to the passenger side and got in. "Answer me, B. Did that nigga do this to you?"

I shook my head yes while trying my best not to slow down on the crying. I had to make sure my story, alongside these bruises, was enough to convince him.

"Yo, what the fuck did he do that for?"

"He found out about you! He kept saying he was going to kill you, and he kept hitting me because I didn't tell him who you were," I cried out.

He reached over and put his arm around me. "Listen, B, I'ma kill that nigga. He has no idea what the fuck he just did, putting his hands on you."

"I don't want him dead; he's my kids' father. I just can't believe he would do this to me." I hugged him tight.

"Ma, I promise you, I've got you. He'll never do this to you anymore. Come on; let me get you to the hospital."

"No, I don't want to go there. I just want to lie down for a little while."

"Damn, I was about to handle something real quick, but I can get you a room at the hotel real quick, get you checked in, and then I'll come back later."

"I thought you stayed somewhere around here. Why can't I go to your house?" I pulled myself away from his hold.

"Ma, I just told you, I was about to handle something. I promise you; you can come over whenever I'm there."

I peeped the nervous look on his face, but I quickly let it go. I was here for something else, something more important to me. I would revisit that situation at another time.

"Listen, babe, don't stress yourself. I'ma handle this nigga and get you out of this fucked-up shit. Let's see how tough this nigga is when he's looking down on the barrel of my gun. I thought you owned a gun."

"I do, but it was in my drawer upstairs. When he first hit me downstairs, when I did get to run up there he had already taken it out of the drawer."

"He's a fuck nigga for real. That nigga gonna feel my wrath. He gon' pay wit' his motherfucking life."

I was very pleased with the way things turned out. I toned the crying down a little bit. "I'm sorry. I didn't mean to bring you into my drama. I just didn't know who else to turn to."

"No, ma. Ain't no need to apologize. I'm your man, and I should've been there to protect you. Matter of fact, I think you need to start looking for a new place. Get away from that fuck nigga."

"I need to have a talk with my girls and let them know that we have to move out," I lied.

"A'ight, good. Now, let's go find this room. You okay to drive? Or do you need me to drive you?"

"I've got it; you can follow me."

He got out of my car and got into his car. I pulled off, and he pulled off right behind me.

I quickly dried my tears, but I couldn't get rid of the pain from the cuts on my forehead. I used my right hand and dug into my purse. I pulled out my bottle of Aleve and took out four pills. I used an old soda I had in the car to wash them down. Hopefully, that would ease the pain a little. I knew it would hurt but, shit, I didn't bargain for this much pain. I felt like my brain was gonna come through my skin at any minute.

I pulled into the parking lot and parked. There was no way I could walk up to the receptionist like this without bringing attention to my face. The last thing I needed was for people to question me about my injuries. I dialed his number and waited for him to respond.

"Yo."

"J, can you get the room? I don't want people to see me like this."

"I've got you! I will let you know, and you can enter through the side door."

I sat in the car, waiting. Ten minutes later, he called me on the phone. I grabbed my purse, locked my car, and snuck in without bumping into anyone.

"Ma, you sure you don't want me to take you to the hospital?"

"I'm sure. I'm gonna take a hot bath and lie down for a little."

"A'ight. I'ma run a few errands. I will be back in a li'l while. Hit my line if you need me." He stepped toward me and hugged me tight.

After he left, I got up and put the lock on the door. I was in my feelings that here I was, all beat up, and this nigga left. What could be so damn important that his ass couldn't stay and take care of his woman?

I took a long bath, thinking of my master plan. I was shocked that little ol' me could actually come up with such a brilliant idea. See, these niggas thought that I was only a great lawyer. They had no idea that I was also a master thinker. Soon enough, they would both find out I was not to be fucked with.

I got out of the shower and cleaned up my wounds with peroxide that I had grabbed earlier out of my medicine cabinet at home. The bleeding stopped, but the swelling was still there. I thought of calling the police to get Trent arrested, but that would be too damn easy. He had half of them motherfuckers in his pocket, so that was useless.

Now that I cleaned myself up, I called room service. I ordered a well-done steak dinner and a bottle of champagne. It was my way of rewarding myself for my brilliant performance. I almost choked, laughing at myself.

I made a mental note to be careful from this point on. I didn't want anyone to know that I was screwing my client. At the end of the day, the dick wasn't worth the problem or the embarrassment that would come down on my law firm and me.

CHAPTER SIX

Malaya

"You are glowing lately. Let me find out you're getting some," Dana joked.

"Who are you talking about?"

"Who else would I be talking about? I've noticed how happy you've been the last few days. I've also noticed the flowers getting delivered daily, and my nosey behind also noticed the young, handsome Mr. Sanders has been popping up without appointments. And, the other day, I saw you getting out of his car and him pulling off."

"Damn, have you been spying on me? You notice a lot of shit." I laughed.

"Hmm, so being the future lawyer I am, I've learned to read people's behavior. So, being the pro I am, I think there is a love connection going on between you and Mr. Sanders." She looked at me.

I thought about lying but decided to let the secret out. After all, this bit of information may become handy one day. "Well, you know I'm married, and I can't let this get out because he is my client. But, yes, Javon and I have been seeing each other. But you know I'm still married, plus he is looking at prison time, so it ain't that serious."

"So, did he tell you about his fiancée?"

"His what?" I gave her a strange look.

"She called the office the other day. She wanted to know what she could do to help his case. She said she wanted to testify because of the charges they brought against him. She was there with him and his children."

She caught me off guard with this shit. This nigga and I talked about lots of shit. How the fuck could he leave out this little bit of information?

"Malaya, you all right? He didn't tell you, did he?"

"Uh, yes, girl. I knew about her. It's no biggie; he's my fuck partner. You know Trent and I have been having our issues, so he was just something to pass the time."

"I hear you talking, but I think y'all are definitely in love with each other. You're my friend, and I don't want you to be hurt, so just be careful.

Sometimes these hood niggas be coming with a lot of drama that you may not be prepared to deal with," she said with a sincere look on her face.

"Thank you for looking out for me, but I'm a big girl, and I can definitely take care of myself." As soon as I said that, I remembered that Trent took my gun away from me. I made a mental note to report it stolen so I could get another one.

"Come on. Let's get back to the office," I said as I got up. Lunch was great, but I was ready to get back to the office.

On the walk back to the office, even though Dana was talking about a bunch of foolishness, my mind was not there. I couldn't wait to get into my office. I couldn't believe this nigga had a bitch and didn't tell me. But, on the real, I had no idea why I was mad. He was my dick on the side, not my man.

I entered my office and closed the door. I quickly sat down and pulled up his number on my cell phone. He didn't pick up, and his voicemail came on. I hit redial, and it started ringing again.

"Yo," he answered without a care in the world.

"So, you've got a woman and didn't tell me?"

"What the fuck are you talkin' about, B?"

"Your fiancée called my office talking about she wants to help wit' your case."

"Man, you trippin.' You may be talkin' bout my baby mama, but you already know about her." He laughed nervously.

"Why in God's name would your baby mama think y'all are engaged? I'm not for no drama or games. You have a bitch; you need to let me know. I'm too grown to be running around with other people's men."

"Ma, listen to me. I done told you, I ain't got no woman. Shit, if I did, I wouldn't be pursuing you the way I'm doing. The only woman I want is you. I'll be happy when your ass gets a divorce from that fuck nigga. Anyways, we goin' finish this later 'cause I'm in the middle of handling something."

I hung the phone up without saying bye. I couldn't say that I fully believed what he was saying to me. I wasn't stupid. If she was his baby mama like he claimed, why was she calling my office to offer her help? I was irritated to my soul because, even though he wasn't my man, we'd been spending a lot of time together; plus, I couldn't have another bitch threatening what I was trying to do.

Javon

I was pissed as fuck when I saw what ol' boy did to my bitch. I knew that was her husband, but I needed her. I couldn't have anything or anybody threatening my well-being. My first thought was to go over there and blow his fucking head off, but I quickly dismissed that idea. I couldn't risk Tania hearing about this. Even though Malaya wasn't my main bitch, I ain't gon' lie, she was growing on me a little. Not only that, this bitch was my only ticket to stay out of prison. I knew that one day, me and that fuck nigga was going to meet and, when we did, it was going to be the day that his life would end.

I was on my way to have a meeting with the crew. For days, I had a lot of shit on my mind. Even though I fucked with these niggas, I had that deep feeling that Abraham was right, and after Malaya told me that they had a confidential informant working with them, that really confirmed it.

We decided to meet up at the new spot, even though I knew that if we had a rat on the team, the police may have already known about it. There was no way I was gonna let these fucking pigs stop my money flow.

I entered the room where they were smoking and drinking. "Yo, what's good, fam?" I said and made sure I make eye contact with every last one of them.

"Whaddup, son?" my partner Mann-Mann asked, and we exchanged dap.

"Yo, the reason why I wanna rap with y'all niggas is because word on the street is that one of you are working with the peoples." I took a pause so I could observe the reaction from each nigga.

"What the fuck you mean? You trying to say that one of us is a fucking rat?" D. Drizzle stood up.

"Yo, my nigga, that's exactly what the fuck I'm saying. I know it ain't me. Yo, ain't nobody knew about the spot that got raided, so how the fuck did the police raid it? Just like they got me on tape talking about certain shit. I don't talk business with no-motherfucking-body but y'all. It's too many coincidences for me to ignore it."

"Yo, I feel disrespected as fuck. From day one, a nigga's been riding with you. I ain't no motherfucking rat, so whoever the fuck it is needs to own their shit 'cause I ain't feeling this shit," Mann-Mann said.

I looked at D. Drizzle; he wasn't saying much. Instead, he was pretending like he was texting on his phone.

"Do you have an idea who it might be?" I looked at D. Drizzle.

"Nah. I 'ont have no idea, son. I know it ain't me, so I ain't gon' point no finger and shit."

It wasn't what he said but how he said it. Here he was, supposedly facing life in prison, and he was acting all nonchalant and shit.

"Yo, word to my mother, if and when I find out who the fuck is working with the motherfucking police, it's gonna be blood every-motherfuck-ing-where."

I was sure it wasn't my other two niggas because they were too thorough to be rats. I knew then, without a doubt, he was the one. I wanted to pull out my gun and splatter that nigga's brain, right then and there, but it wouldn't be a good move. Plus, I didn't know if the police were close by.

"I'm out! My nigga let's roll, go handle some business," I said to my partner.

I got into my truck, and Mann-Mann got in on the passenger side.

"Yo, my nigga, who you think it is?"

"That nigga, D. Drizzle. Before today, I woulda said nah, but I peeped how nervous he was when I was talking, so without a doubt, I know it's him."

"I been peeped that shit since the day we got torn off. He was the first nigga to bond out. I asked who posted his bond, but he ain't said shit. That nigga deserves to die."

"Ain't no other way. It's death before dishonor. And this nigga done betrayed e'erything we stand for."

I was tight as fuck. I wondered how long he'd been working with the police. I knew it wasn't going to be good for us. We did too much dirt together, and this nigga knew too much about the operation. I rubbed my hand over my face. Stress was an understatement to describe the way I was feeling.

"Where we heading to?"

"We gon' follow this nigga. See who he's been talk-ing to."

"Gotcha."

I pulled off and pulled into a spot where no one could see me. I saw when D. Drizzle's car drove by. I slowly pulled off behind him, making sure he did not see me following him.

After days of following him around, I really didn't see any activity, but I didn't care 'bout that. I knew that nigga had to go ASAP. I got dressed and jumped in my Jeep. I was on a mission. I had been up all night; so much shit was going on around me. It was like everything was good just months ago but, here I was, looking at life in prison. I ain't going lie; I wasn't ready. Ain't no way I was going to just let them take me in like that. I cut the music up as the tears rolled down my face. I wasn't crying 'cause I was scared; I was crying because of what I was about to do.

It's amazing to me, homie
that niggas you fuck wit', dawg,
you don't know the truth about these
niggas until
y'all fall out.
The mo' you show a nigga, the mo' dan-
gerous he
become to ya, homie.

I listened to Plies's song, "Kept It Too Real," for the entire ride. I parked my Jeep down two blocks. I tucked my gun in my waist and put my gloves on, and then I crept through the cut that led to D. Drizzle's crib on Thirty-second Street. I wasted no time; I went to the back. I tried the door, and it opened. I stepped inside and looked around. I'd been in there before, so I knew how the house was set up. It seemed like everyone was asleep, which was a good sign for me. I tapped the nigga's door, and he jumped up.

"Yo, boss, what the fuck you doing in here?" He tried to reach for his gun that was on the table.

I took several steps closer and pointed my nine at his head. "Go ahead and try me!"

"Man, you trippin.' What the fuck is going on with you, boss?"

"You already know what this is, my nigga. I hate a motherfucking rat."

"Boss, I swear on my mama that ain't me. You my motherfucking nigga. I would never do no shit like that to you," he pleaded.

"Nigga, fuck you!" I pulled the trigger, firing two shots to his head and two to his chest. I grabbed his cell phone, turned around, and ran out.

"Noooo. Oh, my God. Help," his mother said when she saw me. I grabbed her, threw her against the wall, and fired two shots in her chest, making sure she was dead. I ran through the rest of the house. It was empty, so I quickly snuck back through the door.

I was kind of fucked up that I had to blast his mama also. There was no way I could've known she was in his crib, because she lived in Washington, DC. I remembered how sweet she was to me when I was growing up, but fuck it; there was no way I could leave her alive.

As fast as I got there, I disappeared. I drove all the way out so I could dump the gun. I threw the gun and then lit the gloves on fire. I then got into my Jeep and sped down the highway. I lit a blunt with Plies blaring through my speakers. That was one problem that I didn't have to worry about no more.

Malaya

It was family day with the girls. So much had been going on that I had been neglecting them a little. So, today, I decided to take them out to lunch and then shopping. Regardless of what was going on with their daddy and me, I loved my girls to death.

We ate lunch at Regency Square Mall, and then we went into Macy's. These girls knew how to run my pockets. I ended up spending over $2,000, but it was fine because they were both doing great in school, so they deserved it. We were exiting Macy's when I came face to face with Javon walking toward me, with a chick holding on to his arm.

I stopped dead in my tracks! I looked at him, and he locked eyes with me. I could tell the nigga was just as shocked as I was. "Hey, there, Mr. Sanders."

"Yo. What's good, yo?" he nervously said.

"Babe, who is this?" the bitch asked.

"This is my attorney, Mrs. Ipswich."

"Oh, okay. I think I called your office the other day, and your secretary said she would leave you a message. How rude am I?" She giggled. "I'm Tania, Javon's fiancée."

"Fiancée? Well, congrats, Mr. Sanders. Why didn't you share the good news?"

"He is shy sometimes. You know how these men are." She rubbed his hand.

"Yes, don't I know how these men can be; and oh, yes, I was busy handling your fiancé's case. I think I've got it handled, though. Anyway, I've got to go. It was nice seeing you; and, Mr. Sanders, please call my phone as soon as you're not busy with your family," I said sarcastically. "Come on, girls," I said as I stepped off.

"Mama, who was that? He was looking at you like he was mad or something."

"Baby, that was one of my clients. That's how he looks."

I couldn't tell my daughter that was the nigga I was fucking around with, and that was the bitch he wasn't claiming. I walked to the car, and we got in. I tried not to show it, but I was deeply bothered.

As soon as we got home, I went straight to my room, locked my door, and lay down. I just asked this nigga about this the other day, and he blatantly lied. I needed to get my shit in order. I did not leave my husband to fuck with a nigga who had his own family. I had no idea what the fuck was going on in my life. I needed to get this shit under control.

I wanted to just say fuck this nigga and his fucking case, but I was too deep in it. I loved this fool's dick, and I knew it was too late in the case to go to the judge and let him go. The judge would want to know what was going on, and there's no way I could let him know. I was in too much shit right now. I had to come up with a way to get out of all of this. I'd have rather been myself than to run around here being a nigga's side bitch. For all that, I could have just stayed with my husband.

I should've stayed away from Javon, but I ain't goin' to lie; I missed him eating my pussy and fucking me good. So, I ignored him for a few days, but I couldn't ignore him any longer, so I decided to go and see him. I was still annoyed but, being the bitch I was, I decided not to let my personal feelings get into the middle of what I needed done. So, I swallowed my pride and got into my car.

I entered the room, and he was lying there. "Hey, you," he said. He got up and picked me up.

"What are you doing? Put my ass down."

"Ma, I really need to rap with you. I know you're tight about the other day, but I swear on my dead mama I'm not with that girl. She's just on some other shit. The other day she accused me of sleeping around with you and threatened to take my kids away from me. I can't afford to lose my kids, ma. I was shocked when she said that we were engaged, but I couldn't say anything because I didn't want y'all fighting in the mall, and especially in front of your girls."

"Really? So you were protecting me and my girls' feelings? Bullshit, Javon. I know you're fucking with her, but you ain't got to lie. Just stop playing with my fucking feelings." I pretended like I was really hurting deep inside.

"Ma, come on. I'm that nigga. I can get any bitch in this damn state, but I want you. Ain't none of these bitches in your class. You're in a league by yourself, ma."

There was something about his words that made me feel warm inside. That nigga had a good way with words. Maybe it was the way he looked into my eyes and it seemed like he was talking to my soul. Bitch, quit playing with your overly dramatic ass, a voice in my head said.

After he was done with his rehearsed speech, we ended up fucking—not making love but fucking. He ripped my clothes off and hungrily gave the dick to me, and I threw it back on him. I felt like I was starving for the dick. We went at it for about two hours. We would cum, rest for a few, and then, as soon as his dick got hard again, we were back at it again. I knew damn well the people next door had to hear the headboard banging. I didn't give a damn. I was enjoying myself, and he was too.

After we were finished, we decided to take a shower together, and you'd think we'd be tired. Hell nah. He soaped my body up, and then he slid inside of me from the back. I'm not going to lie; this nigga knew how to satisfy every inch of my fucking body. We spent another twenty minutes in the shower, and then we got out.

We ordered something to eat and lay back and chilled. I thought he was trying to prove to me that he wasn't with that girl. Truth be told, I wasn't tripping off of that shit no more. At the end of the day, he was going to do him, and I was going to do me.

"Hey, babe, my husband is still threatening me. I swear, I cannot take any more from this man. The other day when you said you were going to finish him off, were you serious? I mean, when he beat me up the other day, you said you were going to get rid of him."

"You serious?" He looked at me.

"Yes. I'm so serious. I'm tired of him threatening me and my girls' lives. I want him out of my life, but I don't want to get a divorce because most of the money belongs to me. I don't want to give him a dime of my daddy's hard-earned money." I quickly caught myself.

"You're tripping, B. I mean, you do know this is serious right?" he questioned in a serious tone.

"Yes, I'm a lawyer, so I do know the seriousness, but I'm tired of him beating on me. I'm scared I might kill him myself."

"I need to think about this. I ain't worried about killing no nigga, but this is your husband we're talking about. You have history with this nigga, and he is your kids' father."

"I thought about that too, but he's going to kill me. I can't live like this anymore." I burst out crying. "I wouldn't ask you to do such a horrible thing if I didn't need it done. I know I don't have to worry about you telling anybody."

"How soon are you talking about?"

"I want him gone as soon as possible."

"A'ight, let me think on it. I ain't got no problem finishing this nigga off. I just want to make sure you're serious and won't go back and say I did the shit."

"I'm not no soft bitch. I would pull the trigger my-damn-self, but I know I'm the first person they would look at. I know what I want, and I know I'm tired of him trying to hurt me. If you decide not to kill him, then I will have to do it myself." I cried some more.

"Nah, we wouldn't want you to do that. I need you to be around to defend me. I can't trust my case with nobody else. Like I said, let me think on this, and I will get back wit'cha. Do me a favor; don't text or call me talking about this at all. You hear me?" he said, all serious and shit.

"Yes, I got it." I sniffled.

I was jumping for joy inside. I didn't know it was going to be this easy. I tell you, pussy is a powerful weapon. I knew I was going to have to play the part of the grieving wife. I didn't give a fuck about my husband getting killed. I just didn't want it to come back on me. God knows I couldn't do a day in prison behind no bullshit. I knew Javon was a standup dude, and I knew he would lie down before he snitched on anyone. That kind of loyalty was rare but definitely what I needed.

We end up spending a few more hours together, and then I decided to go home. I had to fix a few things, so I decided to have a talk with Trent.

On the ride home, I started mapping out my plan in my head. I knew that I had to make sure I thought this out and that I was sure that this was what I wanted.

I walked upstairs and knocked on his bedroom door.

"Who is it?"

"It's me. Open up!"

"Bitch, what the fuck do you want?" He leaned his head out the door.

"I just want to talk to you."

"Talk to me? Why should I talk to you, bitch?"

I was sick of being called all these bitches, but I didn't let it get to me; not this time, anyway. "Trent, please! I know we've been going through some things, and I know you probably hate me right now, but I've been doing a lot of thinking, and I just feel like we need to talk."

As soon as the words left my mouth, he opened the door and walked away. I walked inside of what smelled like straight ass and dirty dick. I sat at the edge of the bed, disgusted by the sight of the room. However, I didn't say anything about it.

"Listen, Trent, when I married you it was for better or for worse. Yes, I was hurt when I walked in the room and saw you with that person. You crushed my heart. Trent, you're my husband, my life partner, you're my everything in this world. These past few weeks have been hard for me and, to make matters worse, you put your hands on me. I was shocked my husband was hurting me like this, but I'm willing to put it all behind us if you just try to understand where I'm coming from. Feel my pain. I would've never done this to you, Trent," I cried.

"I told you over and over, I'm sorry. I was dead-ass wrong for bringing that guy up in here, but I'm a man, and I have needs. I can't even touch you. You stopped having sex with me; you stopped talking to me. To be honest, I feel like you had another relationship out there. I got up many days and made your breakfast, cleaned your bathroom, cleaned up the house. I played the bitch in here, trying to please you because I wanted my wife. But the more stuff I'm doing, the more you pulled away. Yes, I'm wrong as hell. I went out there, and I cheated on you. I shouldn't have, and I know that it hurt you when you walked in on us having sex, but I just wanted you to give me a little bit of attention, just a little bit. Let me know you still love me. I want you to love me the way you used to love me. I don't want no other bitch; I want my wife."

I guess you only want niggas, I thought as I looked at this fool performing. "Look, Trent, let's go to counseling and try to get us some help."

He looked at me and took my hand. "You know how long I've wanted this? We can definitely go to counseling and get some help so we can get our marriage back on track."

"I hope you're serious because I can't do this anymore. I've never cheated on you. You know even when you put your hands on me and accused me of being a slut, I never cheated on you, and I have no intention of it. So, you need to get rid of all them niggas, get a new phone, or whatever it is. Let these bitch niggas know that you and your wife are about to work on your marriage."

He hugged me, and I squeezed him back. We ended up talking for a little bit longer, and I left the room. My stomach was sick from having to sit there and listen to his lies.

I was a strong woman, so I put on my big girl's panties and played the loving wife. I had to let my husband know that I loved him, especially if it meant that he wasn't going to be around for much longer. The next couple of days were family days. The girls were happy that their daddy and I were back talking and doing things as a family, just like old times. After the kids went to bed, we would sit up, drinking and talking. I would drink wine, and he would drink whiskey.

It came down to one Friday night. The kids were gone to their grandma's house. He and I were home alone. He reached over and tried to kiss me. At first, my body tensed up, but I quickly caught myself. If I was playing the position, I had to play it all the way out. I allowed myself to kiss him back and, before I knew it, he was on his knees, eating my pussy. I tried with everything in me to enjoy it, but I couldn't, so I started thinking about Javon and how good he ate my pussy. In no time, my pussy was wet, and Trent thought he was doing the damn thing. We ended up having sex, even though the shit was just as boring as it was before. I threw this pussy on him like my life depended on it.

"Baby, please fuck me," I screamed.

"My God! Malaya, I fucking love you," he screamed out.

I didn't say a word; all I knew was that this would benefit me in the long run. I wished he'd just hurry the fuck up. I was also scared because I didn't make him use a condom. I hoped this was the last time I would be screwing this faggot.

Trent eventually moved back into our bedroom. Most nights, I just wanted to go to sleep, but he wanted to make love. I didn't deny sex; in fact, I kept him happy. In my book, we were back to being the loving family we were known to be. I also made sure we went to lots of functions together. For the next few weeks, I played the doting wife who stood proudly beside her husband.

I turned to red wine for comfort, especially when we were having sex. As soon as we were finished, I would run to the bathroom and wash from head to toe. It's sad that I felt this way, but after the way this bastard treated me, I couldn't stomach him. What's funny was that he really thought shit was great between us. He showed no remorse for what he did to me. I didn't let my anger toward him deter me from getting things done.

Javon

Shawty was dead-ass serious when she said she wanted this nigga gone. At first, I thought she was joking, but she was not joking. I knew I said I would murk the nigga, but I soon dismissed that idea. However, she kept bringing it up every day, so I knew I had to get it done. There was something about this that didn't sit right.

"Yo, this lawyer bitch wants me to get rid of her husband," I turned and said to my right-hand man.

"You serious? What that nigga do to her?"

"Yo, he's beating her and the girls."

"Damn, dawg. You sure this bitch ain't playing you? Why would she ask you to do that?"

"One day, he busted up her face, and I saw it. I was mad as fuck, so I told her I was goin' to murk that nigga. But I forgot about the shit, and I thought she did too."

"Hmm. I 'ont know, yo. You my nigga; let me do it if you goin' to do it. You're fucking her, so if anything happens, they're goin' to look at you."

"Man, I 'ont want to bring you in this shit. This my beef."

"Shit, you're my brother, so it is my beef. Don't trust that bitch, though. That's why you should let me handle it."

"A'ight, man; you're right. I'll let you know the details if I decide to carry it out."

I tried to avoid Malaya for a few days, but she kept calling. I already knew what she wanted. I made up my mind to go ahead and have Mann-Mann handle it for me. That way I couldn't be caught up if this bitch decided to renege.

I gave my partner the address and told him the signal to look out for. He was dressed in all-black pants and a shirt with a black hoodie on. He decided to ride out on his motorcycle, just in case he got caught into a situation.

"Man, be easy, and hit me when you're finished." I gave him dap.

"I've got you, partner." He pulled his visor down and rode off into the pitch-dark night.

Malaya

When a woman's been hurt by a man, it's sometimes hard for her to ever forgive him or love him the way she used to love him. I was sure this was what I wanted because there was no other way out of this marriage. Even though we were going to counseling and Trent was being sweet, I knew it wasn't going to last. I was tired of fucking him, and I just wanted it to stop!

I was even more shocked when he told the counselor that he started fooling around with niggas while he was attending college at VSU. I wanted to get up and scream. This nigga had been a faggot for that long, and I had no idea. It took everything in me not to walk out on that session. Instead, I sat there, feeling disgusted as fuck.

Finally, I got word from Javon that everything was going as planned. I was overjoyed that I wouldn't have to go through this foolery for much longer. I decide to cook a big dinner today. I cooked ham, roast beef, yams, rice, and green beans, and I even baked a nice lemon cake. We drank, ate, and laughed like old times. The kids even pulled out some of their old jokes. This was definitely a dinner that we would remember for years to come.

After dinner, I went to do the dishes. "Hey, babe, let me help you clean up the kitchen," Trent whispered as he walked up behind me and kissed me on the neck.

My body shivered but not in a good way. I used everything in me to remain still. "Nah, I've got it. Go relax; I will be up in a minute."

"All righty then. I'll be waiting for you, my love."

I didn't respond; I kept wiping off the counter and putting the dirty dishes in the dishwasher. My nerves were kind of on the edge, so I poured a glass of wine and gulped it down. It took a few minutes, but my nerves were calm. I swept the kitchen and mopped the floor. It had been a long day, and I was beat, but sleeping was the last thing on my mind.

I decided to visit the girls' rooms. I just needed them to know how much I loved them. Now that her daddy and I were back on good terms, Myesha was back speaking to me. I could see that Nyesha was happy also. I just hoped God would wrap His hands around my girls because their world was about to turn upside down. I kissed both of them, gave them a hug, and walked into my room.

"Hey, there you are. I thought you were avoiding Big Daddy." He chuckled.

"Me avoiding you? You know I love a challenge." I winked at him.

"Well, then, come and show me what you're made of."

"Let me bathe first. You sure don't want no dirty pussy," I said as I walked into the bathroom.

I welcomed the water on my tired body. I closed my eyes and daydreamed about Javon fucking me. I stuck my finger into my pussy to grind to the sweet melody of his voice singing in my head. "Awwee," I barely screamed as I worked my fingers inside of my pussy. I rested one foot on the tub as I stuck two more fingers inside of me. My pussy was throbbing, and I delivered. Before I knew it, I exploded on my fingers. I shook uncontrollably as I released my sweet juices from my body. When I was finished, I grabbed my sponge and washed my pussy. By the time I got out of the tub, I was tired but sexually satisfied.

"Damn, you took forever. I would've fallen asleep if it weren't for me wanting to taste that sweet pussy of yours."

I smiled at him, cut the light off, and crawled in the bed. Trent rolled over beside me and started to suck on one of my breasts. I rubbed his head as he started fondling me with his other hand. My goal was to get his dick hard so he could fuck me. He slowly slid his dick inside of me, and I starting winding on it. "That's what I'm talking 'bout, baby. You know how to please your man. Give me this sweet pussy, baby," he said as he long-dicked my pussy.

I hope this shit be over soon.

After he busted, I jumped up off of the bed and ran into the bathroom. I blinked the light twice before I closed the bathroom door. "Don't move, nigga!" I heard a voice say.

"Who the fuck are you, and what do you want?"

There was no response; I heard gunshots. They weren't loud, just light popping sounds.

I waited for about five minutes, and then I opened the bathroom door and ran out. No one was there but Trent's limp body. There was blood all over him. I touched his face; he wasn't breathing.

"No, aw, no, help. Somebody help me," I screamed as I managed to get up and run out of the room. Blood was all over my hands. I ran in Nyesha's room.

"Mommy, what's wrong? Is that blood all on you?" She ran over to me.

"Where's your phone? Call 911. Your daddy is shot, and I need to find your sister."

I ran out of the room and into Myesha's room. She was fast asleep. "Wake up, baby. Pleaseeee. There is an intruder in the house," I yelled.

"What, Mom? What are you talking about?" she yelled.

"Calm down. Someone broke in here and shot your father. Come on."

I grabbed her hand, and we ran into Nyesha's room. She was hiding in the closet. I scooted down in between my girls, and we started to pray.

"Mom, I think I hear the police coming," Nyesha said.

"Let's stay here until they find us. I'm not sure if the intruders are gone."

I heard a commotion downstairs, and then I heard footsteps running up the stairs. "We have one in here. Hello. Is anyone else in here?" I heard a man yell.

"Yes, we're in here. Please help us," I screamed at the top of my lungs.

"It's the police, ma'am. You all are safe now," the officer said as he shined the light on us.

"Thank God you're here. Please go help my husband. Pleaseeeeeeeeeee," I screamed as I collapsed on the officer.

When I finally woke up, I was on the couch in the living room. "Mom, are you okay?" Nyesha asked me.

"Yes. I was feeling dizzy. I think I blacked out for a few seconds."

"Mom, I think Dad is dead." She started to cry.

I moved closer and wrapped my arm around my daughter. Nyesha scooted closer to me and wrapped her hands around my waist. I wished I could take away their pain or explain to them that this was temporary. "God, please give my daughters strength," I whispered.

"Ma'am, can we talk to you and the girls? I know it's hard, but we need to get an idea of what happened here. I'm sorry to inform you that your husband didn't make it. It seemed like he was shot multiple times and died instantly."

"Noooooo! Nooooo! It can't be; it can't be." I started crying with everything in me. I knew that the way I acted would be under scrutiny. "What do you want to know? I'm an attorney, so I know y'all have to question the immediate family."

"What was your husband doing at the time of the shooting?"

"Officer, I would prefer not to answer these questions in front of the girls."

"Sure, I understand. Detective Pelluso will take them to another room."

After the girls were gone, I looked at the officer. "Officer, to answer your question, we had just finished having sex, and I went to the bathroom to clean up. No, I didn't see the intruder's face; and, no, my husband didn't have any enemies I knew about; and, yes, we're having marital problems, but we're in counseling. Yes, you can check me for gunpowder residue."

"You're aware of the law, huh? Oh, you did mention that you were a lawyer. What type of law do you practice?"

"I'm a criminal defense attorney."

"So, you're one of them who gets these bums off when we lock them up," he said sarcastically.

"Officer, no disrespect, but you're here to investigate my husband's murder, not worry about what I do for a living."

"Yes, ma'am. I'm sorry." His smile turned to a dumb frown.

"Okay, Officer, if we're done here, I would like to see my children, plus call my husband's family and inform them."

"Ma'am, first I need you to come with me to identify if this is your husband."

I followed him into my bedroom. His body was in the same place that he was when I last saw him. I took a quick glance and then turned away. "Yes, that's Trent, my husband," I cried.

"Okay, you can go to your girls. They are in the living room area."

I ran downstairs and to my girls. "Girls, I'm so sorry, but your daddy is gone. Our love is gone," I cried as both of them held each other and cried.

"Ma'am, do y'all have any other place to spend the night? Because this is a crime scene now, and investigators will be running in and out all night."

"Yes, we have a few other properties that we can go to."

"Well, I would suggest y'all grab a few things and go. I would like you and the girls to come to the precinct in the morning, so I can get their statement."

"Okay, Officer. We will. Come on, girls. Grab a few things. Myesha, let me see your phone, so I can call your grandmother before she sees this on the news."

I walked outside as the girls gathered a few things. I welcomed the fresh air as it beat down on my face. I felt like all eyes were on me, so I was conscious of everything that I did.

"Hey, Ma; it's Malaya. I'm sorry to call you this late, but your son got shot."

"What do you mean? Where is my Trent?" she yelled into the phone.

"I'm sorry, but he didn't make it. Someone broke into the house and shot him, killing him."

"Nooooooooooooooooo!" was the last thing I heard before the dial tone.

I couldn't imagine what she was going through because he was her only child. Well, all I could do was pray and hope that she would be all right. My only concerns were my children.

I walked back inside. Police were everywhere in the house, gathering evidence. I asked the officer to grab my cell phone out of the room. I wasn't worried about any clothes; I could pick up a few things tomorrow.

The next day was crazier than the day he died. Myesha was inconsolable; I had to take her to the hospital. I felt bad for my child, but she needed to get it under control. Nyesha was handling it much better; she was more worried about my well-being. After they discharged Myesha from the hospital, I dropped them off at home. I called the detective on the case to see if I could go back in the house to grab a few things. He said yes and agreed to meet me at the house.

The minute I stepped foot in that room, I started bawling, and I threw up a few times. There was a big bloodstain in the room. I stepped over it to get to my drawer. I grabbed underwear and a few outfits. The detective consoled me and promised they were going to find my husband's killer.

Javon

I sat in my living room, watching the news. "There was a murder last night in the suburb of Chesterfield. The victim was retired Detective Trent Ipswich . . ."

"Fuck." This dumb bitch didn't tell me her husband was a cop. This wasn't good; that meant the whole fucking force was going to be investigating this killing.

I grabbed my phone and dialed my nigga's number. I was on the edge; I hoped he was good. He picked the phone up.

"Yo, you good?"

"I'm straight, babe. We'll get up tomorrow."

"A'ight, one." I was still tight because I felt like Malaya purposely left out that information, which meant that bitch was on some bullshit. All kinds of thoughts ran through my head; I hoped this bitch didn't set me up.

"Babe, you a'ight? You seem a little bothered," Tania quizzed.

"Nah, I'm good, B," I responded.

"Oh, okay. You didn't have anything to do with that, did you?" she asked.

"Yo, bitch, what the fuck would make you ask me such dumb shit?" I snapped.

"Damn, boy, calm your nerves. I was only playing," Tania yelled.

"Well, that ain't no shit to play about. My name is already in enough shit. I don't need no more. I'm about to bounce."

"Where are you going? Lately, you're always gone. Are you fucking that lawyer bitch? I saw the look on your face the other day when we were in the mall. I'm no fool; I know y'all were both shocked to see the other in the mall."

"Tania, I have no idea what the fuck you're talking 'bout, B. Don't start accusing me of fucking my lawyer. Matter of fact, keep your ass off the phone; quit trying to call that bitch. You fuck my case up, you will regret it," I warned.

"Boy, please, with your idle threats. You keep trusting that bitch. I did some research. You ain't the first dope boy client she's ever fucked, and you definitely won't be the last," she lied.

"Tania, why can't you just shut the fuck up? I told your ass, I'm not fucking this bitch! Now drop it," I yelled.

I got up, grabbed my keys, and stormed out the door. I needed to clear my head and get away from this annoying-ass bitch right now. I jumped into my Jeep and pulled out. I hit my steering wheel to let out all the built-up frustration that I was feeling. All these bitches were riding my nerves. I sure wished this case were over so I could get the fuck on. More and more, Tania was starting to be like one of these annoying-ass bitches out here. She kept thinking a nigga wouldn't walk out on that ass.

I ended up sleeping in my Jeep because I didn't want to hear all that yap, yap, yap. Once in a while, a nigga needs quietness in his life.

It was a long day. We had so much work that we had to get off of us. I was planning to chill out until our cases were over. A nigga wasn't tryin'a catch a new one while on bond. I was about to pull off when Mann-Mann walked outside.

"You leaving?"

"Yeah, about to go collect some money. Yo, how was that shit the other night? E'erything good?"

"Nigga, relax; I do this shit for a living. I went in, handled my business, and was out in less than five minutes. I say this was the easiest kill. As long as that bitch keeps her mouth shut, we're good."

"We ain't got to worry about her saying nothing; plus, she thought it was me. So, your name is definitely not in it. But thanks, yo. I owe you."

"You're good, fam. Be easy out there." We exchanged daps, and I pulled off.

It's kind of strange that I didn't hear from Malaya. Any other day, this bitch would blow up my phone. I dialed Malaya's number. I swear, if I found out that this bitch was playing, I might just kill that bitch after I beat this case.

"Hello. I thought we said we wouldn't call one another."

"Man, fuck that, you're my motherfucking lawyer. Yo, let me ask you a question. Who else you fucking with outside of me?"

"Are you fucking serious? You know what I'm dealing with right now?"

"Man, for real, I 'ont give a fuck 'bout that right now. You wanted that shit, so quit acting like you mourning and shit."

"You need to quit being stupid. I'm here trying to get my girls settled. They are going through a hard time."

"Man, where the fuck you at? I need to see you."

"I'm at the other house, and the girls are here, so I don't think it's a good idea."

"Listen, ma, I want to see you, so run that address and stop bullshitting for real."

This bitch played too much. She was acting suspicious. I wonder if she had one of them niggas she was fucking over there. I wanted to see her so I could feel her out. I was a street nigga; I knew how to pick up on people's behavior, a skill I learned from being around grimy niggas my entire life.

"Javon, are you drinking? You're acting crazy; this is so not you."

"Malaya, I ain't tryin'a hear all this shit. Save all the drama for the courtroom."

"A'ight, I'll text you the address. You can't come inside and only for a few minutes," she said with an attitude.

I drank the last bit of liquor that was in a bottle I had stashed in here and checked my phone. I pulled up the address. I then programmed it in my GPS.

CHAPTER SEVEN

Malaya

What have I gotten myself into? I thought I told this nigga to chill out, but his hardheaded ass wasn't trying to do that. He shocked the hell out of me when he called my phone. I didn't want anyone to know that I was fucking with him. Shit, I kind of regretted telling Dana about him. She was my girl, though. I didn't think she would say anything to anyone. Well, that's what I hoped for anyway.

I heard the phone ringing. I swear if this nigga doesn't leave me the fuck alone . . . What the fuck does he want now? I thought as I grabbed my phone up. I quickly realized that it wasn't him. My heart sank. I hated talking to this bitch.

"Hello," I said dryly.

"So, what did the police say happened?" this rude bitch said.

"Say about what?" I answered with annoyance.

"Malaya, how did someone break up in there and kill my son, and you and your children were not hurt? I don't have any proof right now, but I know you got my son killed. It's mighty funny how you've been treating him lately, and now he dead."

"Listen, lady, I don't want to disrespect you, but before you start accusing me of doing anything to your son, please get your facts straight. I had nothing to do with your son getting killed." I was ready to hang up on this old bitch. She was the reason why her grown-ass son acted the way he did; because she was always supporting that bullshit.

"You are a sneaky bitch! You fool everybody, hiding behind them damn suits and pretending like you're all high and mighty. You never had me fooled; I see you for the trash you really are. I just wish my son had seen it earlier; he would still be here with us today. I will not rest 'til you pay for this. I don't know how you did it as of yet, but I will not rest until I find out."

"Go to hell, you old bitch. Better yet, go join your motherfucking dead son."

I didn't wait for a response. I hung up in that bitch's face. How dare she accuse me of some shit that she knew nothing about? Shit, I didn't kill that nigga. I just helped put that nigga out of his misery.

"Who was that on the phone? Was that my nana?" Myesha asked while she gave me a dirty look.

"Yes, that was your nana," I said as I walked off on her. I wasn't inconsiderate. I knew my daughter's pain was genuine, and now wasn't the time to dig into her ass. So, I did the grown woman shit and walked away.

I decided to take a quick shower because Javon was on his way, and anything was liable to happen. I knew I couldn't take him in the house because that child of mine was patrolling like she was the gotdamn sergeant. I wished she were more like Nyesha: laidback.

I got out of the shower and put on tights and a wife beater along with a pair of flip-flops. My hair needed to be done, but it fit the situation right now. After all, I just lost my husband, the love of my life. I put a little lip gloss on my lips. I didn't want to totally look rough around this nigga.

I heard my phone ringing. I grabbed it. "Hello."

"I'm pulling up."

I pressed End and walked out of my room. I was happy that Myesha's happy ass was in her room by now. I opened the door and stepped outside. I saw him pull in. I looked far behind him to see if anyone followed him. I didn't see anyone, so hopefully no one did.

He got out of the car and walked toward me. "Yo, ma. What's good wit' you?"

"You know you're trippin', right? This is how people get torn off on cases."

"Man, you're my lawyer. We're discussing my case."

I could smell alcohol on his breath. "Javon, were you drinking? What is going on with you lately? You're so different from when we met; you carried yourself differently. I swear I don't like the new you."

"Man, whatever, B. I'm that same nigga you met, but you've got to understand that I'm under a lot of pressure. I'm the head nigga, so everything falls on me. You feel me?"

"No, I don't feel you! It's not clicking in your head that you are in a lot of shit. I told you to try to plead out, but you chose not to. I mean, I have my investigators on the case, but I've seen the evidence. It doesn't look good, and they've got a CI who's gonna testify if y'all go to trial."

"Well, that nigga ain't going to testify against anyone. That nigga is dead."

"What do you mean? You knew who the informant was?"

"Yes, it was my nigga D. Drizzle. That nigga ain't never coming back."

I stood there, looking at him. I was shocked at what he was telling me. "Do you know what the hell you're saying? You're already in some deep shit, and you went and did some more dumb shit."

"Damn, if all they have is a nigga telling and there's no nigga, then they have no case."

"They have more than that. They have your voice; they have pictures of you doing all kinds of shit. They have solid evidence. I'm telling you, I'm not God. I can only do my best, but you're not helping yourself if you're out here still selling drugs and killing people. Who the fuck do you think they're gonna look at now that this boy is dead? You." I poked him in his chest.

"Yo, this is the streets, but I don't expect you to understand. You're from up in the 'burbs; you 'ont know what it is to be hungry day in and day out. You were born wit' money, you never had to struggle, so how the fuck you gonna talk to me about how a nigga's living?"

"You're right. I've never been through none of that shit, but even though I have money, I still get up every day and go to work, working a nine to five, trying my best to get niggas like you off. Stop making excuses. You have plenty money;

you could've left the streets. You need to man up and take responsibility for your actions."

"Look what we have here. How are you different? You just begged me to kill your husband because your ass was too greedy and didn't want him to get a dollar if you divorced him. You ain't no better than me. The only thing is that you're a coward; you couldn't do it. You had to get someone else to handle your dirty work. So, before you come at me, let that sink in."

"You know what? I'm too close to you and this case. There's no way I can continue being your lawyer."

"You ain't got a choice. You've got to defend me. Be careful; you might not like how this shit turns out. I fucks wit' you and all, but my freedom means much more to me than a piece of pussy."

"You know what? Fuck you, Javon. How dare you threaten me? Trust me; you better be careful," I said and walked off into the house. I locked the door behind me and leaned on the door.

"So, Mother, who was that? Oh, let me answer that. That is the same dude from the mall. Right?"

"Little girl, what the fuck is your problem? Why are you breathing down my neck?" I said in a higher tone than I intended.

"I'm just saying, I saw how he looked at you that day at the mall and now my daddy just got killed, and he's paying house visits. Something isn't adding up."

"If you don't get your little fast ass out of my face your teeth ain't gonna be adding up soon. Get your ass somewhere and sit down. I get it; you're hurting from your daddy getting killed, but we're all hurting. You're not the only one."

She must have seen the seriousness on my face because she walked off with an attitude.

I lay in the bed. It was early, but I needed some peace and quiet. My phone had been ringing nonstop since Trent was killed. I just wanted to ignore them all, but I had to play the loving wife who was mourning her wonderful husband's death. I would be happy when all this shit was over.

After taking a week off, I decided to go back to work. I had some cases to go over, plus I needed to get out of the house. Even though that was our second home, everything inside reminded me of Trent. Even the sheets smelled like him. To make matters worse, I kept seeing his dead image in my head.

I also missed Javon fucking me. I was horny as fuck and wanted to feel his dick inside of me.

I knew he was mad about the argument we had that day he came to the house. I'm going to be honest; the nigga was a hothead. I thought he would calm down a little, but the more I dealt with him, the more I realized that the nigga was going to go down hard. I wasn't no hood chick or no ride or die bitch, so I definitely wasn't ready to start riding for a nigga who was heading for derailment if he didn't change the way he carried himself.

The phone started ringing, and I picked up. "Hello."

"Mrs. Ipswich, there are two detectives here to see you," Dana said, almost killing me.

Detectives? Breathe. You've got this, I coached myself. It caught me off guard, but I wasn't surprised. I put my game face on and braced myself for what was about to go down.

"All right. Send them in, Dana."

I closed my computer and turned my phone on to record. I was an attorney, so I was ready for any- and everything. I straightened my blouse and braced myself for what was to come.

"Come in, Detectives." I stood up.

"Hello, again, Mrs. Ipswich. How are you doing today?" Detective Rosales asked.

"I'm doing the best I can under the circumstances."

"Well, the coroner's report is back and, as we already know, your husband was shot three times. The first bullet killed him upon impact. We're trying to follow up to see if you remember anything that you didn't mention to us," Rosales said.

"No, I told you all everything. We just finished having sex. I went to the bathroom to wash up. A person entered the room, told my husband not to move, and then he shot him. My husband was an officer; did you look into his old cases? You know, he locked plenty of thugs away."

"Yes, we are not leaving any stones unturned. Somebody, somewhere, knows something. I couldn't help but notice that the house has an alarm on it. Did the alarm go off? I don't remember seeing that in the report," Detective Pelluso said with a suspicious look plastered across his face.

"No, the alarm was not on. My husband was usually the last one to check all the doors and windows, and he also set the alarm before coming to bed. Like I just told you, I left my husband in the bed and went to take a shower. My husband is usually the one that locked the house up at night, so I assumed he locked up. I had no reason to think he didn't."

"I've got you." He wrote something down in his notepad.

"Mrs. Ipswich, I spoke to the victim's mother, and she kind of hinted to us that you and the victim were having marital issues. Can you elaborate on that for me?" Detective Rosales asked.

"Detective, the first time we spoke, I was very blunt about the issues my husband I were having. And as far as that old bitch, she never liked me. Months ago, my husband cheated on me, but I forgave him, we went to counseling, and were back to being in love again."

"Oh, I understand, ma'am. Do you have the name of the counselor?"

"I do, but am I a suspect in my husband's death?" I stood up.

"No, ma'am, but we have to check out everything and eliminate people from the equation."

"Detectives, I loved my husband. I had no reason to kill him. We are well off, but you can check it out; it's my money. If I wanted to be done, I would've gotten a divorce."

"Mrs. Ipswich, something doesn't smell right. I can't put my fingers on it as of yet, but I will. I suggest that if you know anything, please tell us now."

"With all due respect, Detective, I don't give a damn what you think is going on. Please do your

Tania, I swear, ma, I love you, but if yo[u] [co]ntinue like this, I can't be with you. I do[n'] [k]now how my case is gonna end up and, inste[ad] [o]f supporting a nigga, all you wanna do is fig[ht.] [I] need you, ma; I need my seeds. Stand by yo[ur] [n]igga for once."

"I love you too, but I can't sit back and watc[h] [y]ou carry me over no bitch who doesn't giv[e] a fuck about you. I'm the bitch who was ther[e] when you ain't had shit. So, how the fuck do yo[u] think it feels when a bitch comes from nowher[e] and wants to snatch you up?" she cried.

There was something about her tears tha[t] melted my heart. Even though I was a hoo[d] nigga, I still loved shawty; but Malaya wa[s] beneficial to me right now. The truth was tha[t] both of them had some good pussy. If I could, [I] would love to have both of them. I knew it wasn['t] possible, so I'd have to continue slinging thi[s] dick to both of them.

I ended up eating that pussy up really goo[d] [a]nd laying the dick down. By the time I left th[e] [ho]use, shorty was fast asleep. Yeah, I rocke[d] [th]at ass to sleep.

I decided to hang out with my nigga, Man[ny] [M]ann. It'd been a minute since we kicked bac[k] [an]d rapped. I thought he was taking thes[e] [cha]rges extra hard because he just had a bab[y]

job and find that bum who took my husband away from us. I'm a lawyer, so I know how y'all operate when it's one of you who is killed. But I promise you're barking up the wrong tree. And, since I know how y'all operate, from now on y'all can contact my lawyer."

"Mrs. Ipswich, you're not behaving like a grieving wife. More like a suspect. What do you have to hide? Why are you lawyering up?"

"If you have no other questions for me, I would love for you all to leave. Please see my lawyer with any further questions." I handed him a card.

"Have a great day, ma'am. I promise you will see us again."

"Don't count on it, Detective. Fucking with me will get your badge taken." I winked at him.

As soon as they walked out of the door, I locked the door behind me. I let out a long sigh. My day was going good, but that shit just went to the left. I sat down on my seat, my mind in overdrive. I didn't like that they took that long-ass drive from Chesterfield County to come all the way out here in the city. I didn't like this at all. I sat at my desk, rubbing my temples. I needed a fucking drink, right now.

"Dana, come in here, please."

"Yes. You all right? What's going on? Is everything okay?"

"I need you to call and cancel my appointments for the rest of the day. I just need to get out of here."

"Okay. Is there anything else that you need me to do for you? You know I'm here for you."

"Thanks, hon, but I'm good. I just need to get home."

"Okay, I've got you covered."

I logged out of the Internet and grabbed my briefcase and my purse. I hurriedly walked out of the office. I needed to talk to Isiah. He was a great friend and a great lawyer.

I got into my car and threw my briefcase on the back seat. I sat in the parking lot for a good five minutes, just thinking. Either these motherfuckers know something or they were fishing. Either way, I needed them to leave me the fuck alone. I dialed Javon's number but quickly hung up. I was feeling paranoid. I wasn't sure if his phone was bugged, and the last thing I needed was for them to have me on tape discussing some damn murder.

Obeying a speed limit was not on my agenda today. I couldn't care less about a speeding ticket. I needed to get to my lawyer's office.

Javon

"You think I'm stupid! I know you're fucking with that bitch. The other day when you stormed

out of here, your ass didn't know that [...] you all the way to that bitch's house."

"What? You followed me? Why the fu[...] you do some crazy shit like that?"

"Boy, you're worried about why I followe[...] If you weren't lying and cheating, I wo[...] have to follow your ass. Ever since that [...] started working on your case, you've been a[...] funny as hell. Many days you claimed you w[...] at the trap, but I knew better than that. I sw[...] to God, you keep fucking around with that bitc[...] I'm going to report her ass to the bar association[...]

I grabbed her by the neck and threw her u[...] against the wall. "What the fuck is your proble[...] B? You think I want this bitch, huh? Wrong [...] don't want this bitch; I keep her ass close [...] I can get her to do whatever the fuck I w[...] Nothing more, nothing less." I shoved her [...] until she fell to the ground.

"So, you have to fuck her? What type [...] deal is that? You've got to pay this bitch an[...] her dick? Boy, quit lying."

"I ain't goin' to keep arguing with you, [...] better stay the fuck away from her. I swe[...]

"If I don't, what the fuck are you go[...] You're gonna beat my ass over this bit[...] is it? Is it because this bitch has a fe[...] more than me? Huh? What is it?" She [...] my shirt.

'bout three months ago. If anybody knew him, they knew how bad he wanted a son. As fucked up as everything seemed, we all knew the risks we faced out here in the streets.

I pulled up to Club Infuzion. I saw his Magnum parked, so I parked beside him. I walked in and quickly spotted that nigga. How could I miss him? This nigga was always dressed in New York Knicks apparel from head to toe. Win or lose, he was a diehard Knicks fans.

"My nigga, what's good?" We exchanged daps.

"I'm breathing, my nigga."

I took a seat beside him by the bar. "Ay, let me get a shot of Henney," I said to the bartender.

"So, what's good, fam? How's it looking on your end?" I asked.

"Shit don't look good for real. I rapped with the lawyer today; she tried to get me a plea deal, but the motherfucking state is only offering a minimum of twenty-five years, and I would have to give them everything on you and take the stand on you, my nigga," Mann-Mann said.

"Word!" I replied.

"I told that bitch to tell that nigga fuck him and to take that shit and blow it out his ass. I ain't no motherfucking rat, plus you're my motherfucking bro. Ain't no rolling over, my nigga. Death before dishonor," he responded.

If this shit were coming from another other nigga, I would say bullshit, but this nigga and I had been rolling since we were five years old. We done fucked bitches together, robbed niggas together, and made money together. I knew he loved me just as much as I loved him.

"My nigga, it's sticky as fuck. I'm just betting on this bitch working her powers and shit to get me out. If I'm found guilty, I've got a few things to try to pull out."

"I feel you, my nigga. My girl's not taking it too good; she's talking 'bout running and shit, but I can't leave my seed and her for real. Yo, I forgot to ask you, what the fuck happened to that nigga, D. Drizzle?" he asked.

"I told you, it was death before dishonor. I popped up over there and burned that nigga."

"But damn, dawg, you could've let the mama live, though."

"I never told you I killed the mama. How did you know that?" I asked suspiciously.

"Oh, shoot, I think I caught that shit on the news. You know my girl is always watching the news."

"Oh, okay." I laughed. I was paranoid as fuck. "Hell nah. That bitch ran out there, so I ain't have no choice but to murk her ass too. I would've been a fool if I let her live."

"Yeah, true dat. I just can't kill nobody's mama. I've got a little heart in me."

"Yo, fuck a heart. That bitch knew her son was a motherfucking rat."

"Well, in that case, fuck that nigga and that bitch then." He went back to sipping on his Heineken.

The rest of the night, we drank, smoked, and reminisced on good ol' times. Happier times when we didn't have any cares in the world. Them days were long gone now. Both of us were sitting and hoping things worked out in our favor. The more I thought about how much time I was facing, the more I drank.

At around 12:00 a.m., I was ready to bounce. It felt good to be out and about.

"A'ight, my nigga, be easy."

"A'ight, bro, love you yo." I gave him dap, and we both got into our cars.

I wasn't in any shape to drive, but I wasn't going to call Tania. It was too late for her to pack up the kids and come get me. I fumbled around and found my phone in my pocket. I started to call Malaya but instead decided to pop up over there. It was kind of strange that she wasn't calling me every day like she used to.

I pulled into the driveway, and then I dialed her number. "Hello," she whispered.

"Yo, I'm outside. Open the door."

"What are you doing here? What time is it?"

"I 'ont know, shit. 'Bout one a.m."

"We shouldn't be doing this. It's not safe."

"Girl, chill out and open the door." I hopped out of my car and stumbled to the front door.

She opened the door, and I walked in. "Why are you doing this? My kids are here," she whispered.

"Baby, I had to see you. I miss you so much." I grabbed her, pulled her closer, and stuck my tongue down her throat. She didn't resist, so I knew then that she wanted this dick. "Baby, I want to fuck. Come ride this dick."

"Be quiet. I don't want my kids waking up."

She led me into the basement where there was a couch. I wasted no time stripping her clothes off and throwing her on the couch backward. I dug my face into her pussy, sticking my tongue deep into her ass. I then sucked on her clit. I knew how to please her, and tonight was no different.

"Come ride this dick, baby." I got up off of my knees and lay on the coach. Shawty wasted no time. She got on my rock-hard dick and squeezed her clit together as she slid up and down on my pipe. I felt the urge to bust, but I tried not to. I wanted to enjoy the feeling a little bit. She started to bounce real hard, and I grabbed her hips and pulled her down on my dick.

"Arrghhhh," I growled loud as I exploded in her. "I fucking love you, ma. I love you," I repeated myself. I held her down for a few more seconds, and then I loosened my grip. I was too tired and weak to move. I just lay there until I dozed off.

Malaya

Tomorrow was my husband's funeral, so I was up late, making sure everything was in order. My mind was all over the place. Everything I heard made me jumpy. For some reason, in my crazy mind, I thought the police were watching my every move. Some might say I was acting like a guilty woman by getting an attorney, but I was a smart bitch. I knew how the system worked, and I wasn't going to be railroaded into making a confession.

I allowed his mother to deal with the morgue. The bitch was happy to do so. I wasn't paranoid or anything like that, but I didn't want to deal with his dead ass at all. I paid the money, and she dealt with the rest of it.

This man lost his mind, popping up like that. I was kind of happy to see him, even though it was risky for him to come to the house. I tried to tell him no, but him being the dude he was, he wasn't going for that. At all. I got up, threw my robe on, and tiptoed to the door. I was careful not to wake the girls up. They had a big day ahead tomorrow. Plus, Myesha didn't need to see him in this house. She had been talking to her grandma, and God knows what she done planted in her head.

No matter how much I said I didn't want to see this dude, or lied to myself that I didn't want him, all that changed when we were face to face. His masculine scent did something major to my insides. When he started kissing me, I couldn't resist. I wanted him; I wanted to feel him up inside of me. After everything that has been going on, I welcomed getting my clit sucked on and my pussy beat up. My pussy was thirsty for his dick, and I wasted no time devouring all nine inches with my pussy. I saw that he was enjoying himself, which motivated me to grind a little harder. I was also enjoying myself. My pussy muscles tightened as I came all over his dick. I was even more excited when his dick got larger, and his veins popped out. Without hesitation, he exploded inside of me. This was his first time fucking me without a condom and, I had to say, me feeling his skin inside of me made the sex so much more enjoyable.

He kind of threw me off when he told me he loved me. I turned my lips to say it back, but the words wouldn't come out. I was never in love with him; I just loved the way he fucked me good. At this point in life, I didn't really give a fuck about love. I needed a nigga who respected me and fucked me good. All that love shit isn't what it's hyped up to be.

I could see he was drunk because, about five minutes after sex, he was out. I took a blanket and threw it over him. I was going to let him lie there to kind of sleep off the alcohol, but his ass would have to go before the girls woke up.

I left him in the basement and took a shower. I also started prepping the food. My family would be here in the morning to help out. Even though it was under these circumstances, I was happy I was getting to see my mama and my sisters. I hated that they moved to Maryland and we barely saw each other.

I didn't realize how tired I was until I jumped out of my sleep and looked at the time; it was 6:00 a.m. I jumped up off of the couch and ran downstairs.

"Javon, get up. Get up," I said as I shook him.

"Huh? What?"

"Get up. You need to go before the girls get up."

"Why? Shit, don't you think it's about time they meet me? I mean, we've been with each other for a while now, and I ain't met nobody in your family. Shit, let me find out I'm a secret."

"It's too early for your shit, Javon. My girls just lost their dad, so please have a little heart. And you're nobody's secret, but how the hell do you think it would look if I pop up with a man soon after my husband got killed? I see you don't use your head. From now on, let me do the thinking."

He didn't respond. He sat up and grabbed his shoes. I walked up the stairs, and he followed me.

We were halfway to the door when Myesha stepped out in the hallway. "What is he doing in my daddy's house? He spent the night here?" She stepped closer with her arms folded.

"Little girl, watch your damn mouth."

"No, Mother. My daddy just got killed, and you're already sleeping around; or were you sleeping around before he died? Which one is it, Mom?"

Slap! Slap! "Don't you ever talk to me like that. Javon is a friend. He wasn't feeling good and needed somewhere to chill for a few hours. You're a child, so please play your position."

"I hate you! I know you had Daddy killed! I hate you, Mother," she said as she stormed off.

I opened the door, and we walked outside. "Yo, ma, my bad."

"It's fine. This was the reason why I told you we needed to be careful."

He hugged me, and I walked back into the house. I stood at the counter, and I broke down. So far I'd been trying to hold everything together but, sometimes, it just got to be too much.

"Mama, you okay?" Nyesha's voice startled me.

I quickly wiped my eyes and turned around, facing her. "Baby, I'm just missing your daddy. I wish he were still here with us. Your sister is accusing me of doing something to him." I started to cry again.

A few hours later, the doorbell started to ring. I knew it was my mother and my sisters. I quickly opened the door. "Mamaaaaaaaaaaaa," I screamed as I hugged the woman who gave me birth and who was also my rock when I needed someone to lean on.

"Hey, baby. How are you?" She hugged me tight.

"Y'all come in," I used my hand to call them all in.

"Hey, sissy. I miss you," my little sister, Sophia, said.

"Hey, big sis." I hugged my big sis.

"Where are the girls at?"

"Myesha and Nyesha, your grandma is here," I yelled.

I ended up making breakfast, and we sat down at the table to eat. I sure missed those days when we were one big family. I stared at Mama. That woman had not aged one bit. When all of this was over, I thought I might try to move to Maryland with them.

The day was finally here when I got to say good-bye to Trent Ipswich. I never thought this day would come. When I married him, I thought we would grow old together. For the first part of our marriage, he was everything a woman dreamed of; but then his ass got comfortable and started fucking and sucking everything. My eyes got a little misty. I quickly dabbed them with my washcloth. I continued putting on my makeup.

I was dressed in a long Vera Wang gown with a pair of Jimmy Choo pumps. I knew it was a funeral, but I was pretty sure that some of these hoes he was fucking would be present, and I had a statement to make. I hated to sound conceited, but I would put money on it; I was the best thing that ever happened to him. His mama's ass knew that, and I really thought that was the reason why that bitch didn't like me. I wasn't going to worry about what an irrelevant bitch thought of me. Her son was dead, and she ain't have nothing coming to her but the measly twenty grand he left in his will for her. Everything else was left for his daughters and me. I was a lawyer, so life insurance was definitely up to date. Ain't no way I was going to walk away from this without anything.

Everyone was already outside in the cars. I set the alarm and locked the door. I got in my car. Myesha decided to drive with her auntie, which was good because I wasn't in the mood for that child. "You ready?" I said to Nyesha and rubbed her arm.

"I think I am," she said and gave me a sad look.

"Baby, I love you. Just know that even though your daddy is gone, you will always have your mama."

"I know, Mama, and I love you too."

God, please help me to get through this day. All these fake-ass bitches up in here. The parking lot was already packed, which was expected because the entire police force was out, plus the surrounding police officers were out in full force. I parked and got out. I took my daughter's hand, and we walked in together. I felt all eyes on me as we walked to the front. I held my head high and walked past them. I took my seat in the front, alongside my daughters. His mama and her family were sitting behind me. I didn't turn back to acknowledge this bitch or her fucked-up-ass family. I just prayed that they stayed in their lane because I would hate it if she pushed me today and I had to show my ass off.

> Rock of Ages, cleft for me,
> Let me hide myself in Thee;
> Let the water and the blood,
> From Thy wounded side which flowed,
> Be of sin the double cure;
> Save from wrath and make me pure.

The hymn blasted through the church's speakers. I got up and walked over to the casket. I looked down at Trent. I thought I would've felt some kind of way, but I didn't. I bent down to the corpse, kissed him on the cheek, and whispered, "I love you, Trent, but I hope you rot in hell." I couldn't take the sight of him anymore, so I turned away and walked back to my seat. My head started feeling dizzy. "Trenttttttttttttttt," I screamed out before I collapsed on the floor.

I was conscious. I was just feeling weak, or was it that they were waiting for a performance so I had to deliver? "Get an ambulance," I heard my mama yell.

"No, Mama; I'm good. I'm just a little weak. Just help me get to my seat please."

Mama and Nyesha both held on to me as I walked to the pew. I glanced at his family before I sat down and I realized that them bitches didn't even move an inch to check on me to see if I was fine. I sat down and started crying uncontrollably. I wasn't crying over that bastard. I was crying tears of joy. Joy that I was no longer in prison. I was now a free, single woman.

This ceremony was torture. This pastor stood up preaching about what a good man Trent was. Mind you, this nigga never met my husband, and Trent was nothing close to what he was preaching. The worst part was when his mama got up there, talking about what a great man her son was. I mean, come the fuck on. What was so fucking great about a two-timing woman beater? I rolled my eyes at her; I didn't give a fuck anymore. I was hoping for this charade to be over ASAP so I could get the fuck on with my life.

Finally, the funeral was over. His mama was in her feelings that I decided not to bury him beside his father in their family plot. Too bad. I was the motherfucking wife, and I called the shots. A few people walked up to me, paying their respects. I gladly thanked them for coming. I watched as the family exited the church. I stayed behind to thank the rental-pastor and also slide him $2,000 for a job well done.

I was about to exit the church when his mama stepped in my path. "You think you're gonna get away with this, but you're not. The police are on to you, and I will be right there when they arrest your ass."

"Listen to me, you old bitch. Get the fuck out of my way before you end up joining your dead son. Be careful with those empty threats. It's a wicked world out here." I pushed her out of my way.

"Myesha told me about that man you had at the house. I will be passing on that info to the police," she yelled as I stepped outside.

I was furious when she said that. That fucking daughter of mine was definitely getting on my last nerves. I should have found her and choked her grown ass, but I decided to wait until after the funeral.

CHAPTER EIGHT

Javon

My court case was steadily coming up. I ain't goin' to lie; a nigga was kind of nervous. See, in these streets, I was the motherfucking nigga; but up in the courtroom, these cracker niggas were in control. I was going in here like a real nigga, and I was gonna fight until the end.

I dialed my partner's number, but his phone went straight to voicemail. I hung the phone up, but something about it was bothering me. I hadn't heard from him since the day we kicked it, which was a few days ago. When I stopped by the spot yesterday, he wasn't there, and the niggas claimed they hadn't heard from him either. Man, I hoped my nigga was a'ight. I knew he was under a lot of pressure, but I didn't think it was anything major.

I busted a U-turn and headed toward his house. Thoughts of suicide popped in my head, but I quickly dismissed them because my nigga was a thoroughbred. I knew he wasn't no weak nigga. I kind of felt guilty bringing him into these streets, but there was no one else I felt like I could trust.

I pulled up at his crib and quickly noticed furniture sitting on the curb. I parked and got out. I walked to the side where his Magnum was usually parked, but it was gone, and his girl's car was not there. I turned to walk away, but something told me to walk up on the porch. There were no curtains in the window. I peeped inside and was alarmed when I saw that the place was empty. This was really strange because he bought this house about two years ago. Where did my nigga go? And why didn't he tell me he was moving?

Confused and kind of thrown off, I walked back to my car. I saw the next-door neighbor raking up his leaves, so I hopped out of the car and jogged toward him. "Ay, my man, I was looking for my partner, Mann-Mann, but it seems like they moved."

"I was thinking the same thing; they kind of moved suddenly. One night, my wife woke me up because there were some noises coming from next door. I grabbed my gun and peeped out the window. That's when I saw them moving things into a big U-Haul truck. So, I figured they sold the house."

"A'ight. Thank you, man," I said and walked off.

I was thrown off by everything. This was my brother from another mother. None of this shit made sense. I scrolled through my phone and pulled up his girl's number.

"You've reached a number that's either been disconnected or changed. If you feel like you've reached this recording in error, please dial again."

I hung up and then dialed his number. A few hours ago, it was going to voicemail. Now, it was saying disconnected also. I shook my head in disgust. Something in me told me that shit was wrong. I couldn't put my finger on it, though.

Malaya

I pulled Myesha's ass to the side as soon as we got home.

"What are you doing?" she said as I tightened my grip on her arm.

"Sit down and shut up." I shoved her ass down on her bed. "What is your fucking problem? Your grandma told me what you were over there saying."

"I don't care what Grandma told you. It's the truth!"

"You little bitch! How dare you run over there and tell them some shit about me. You know that old bitch doesn't like me."

"You run around here acting like you're mourning Daddy's death, but it's all for show. You don't miss him."

I looked at her evil ass and thought about strangling her ass, but regardless of how much I despised her right now, she was my child. I looked at her and shook my head. Six more years and I want her out of my house and out of my damn life, I thought before I walked out of the room.

After burying Trent, I decided to go through the house and put all his things together. I was nice enough to hit his mother up to see if she wanted her son's belongings.

"Hello. I'm going through your son's things, and I wanted to know if you wanted his things?"

"You have some nerve calling my damn phone. You can't pack his things up; he's barely in the ground."

"Listen, woman, I'm sick of your ass already. Either you get this damn shit, or I will donate it to the homeless shelter."

"I told my son not to marry your ass. Oh, Lord, I wish he'd listened to me."

"I'm losing my patience with your ass. None of that shit matters. He's dead now, so he won't be with anybody. I'm done dealing with you. You will be hearing from my lawyer with regard to the few dollars he left you."

"Go to hell. You won't be around to spend a dime of my son's money. You will be locked away in a prison cell," she spat.

I'd had it with this old, disgruntled bitch, so I hung the phone up. I should've had her ass killed too because Lord knows she was riding my damn nerves.

I continued throwing all of his belongings in a bag. It wasn't that much because after I bleached all of his clothes he never got around to replacing his wardrobe. When I was finished, I called the Salvation Army. Fuck that ungrateful bitch. She ain't getting shit.

I packed up my things and called the movers. I was putting my belongings in storage until I decided what I wanted to do. I wasn't sure if I wanted to buy a new house or move to Maryland, closer to my family. It would look kind of suspicious if I just up and left, so I decided to hang around.

I decide to move to a house that Trent and I owned; it was smaller, and it wasn't something that I had plan on living in. It was more of an in-

vestment property. I took one last look around;
I used to love this house. This was my home, but
after everything that I endured in here, it was
like prison now. Oh, well, time to move on, I
thought as I walked out the door. I would call
the cleaning crew so they could come out and
clean up the place. I planned on removing the
carpet in the bedroom; some of Trent's blood
spilled all over my off-white carpet. This nigga
was always leaving his damn mess everywhere
he went. I made a mental note to contact my
Realtor so he could get the house on the market
as soon as possible.

My family went back home to Maryland. I
was back at work, and my life was finally back
to normal. I thought everything would be fine;
daytime was all right but, at night, when I tried
to go to sleep I couldn't. I would fall asleep but,
right after, I kept seeing Trent's dead face. I
would try to block it out, but I couldn't. I wasn't
sad that he was dead, so why did I keep seeing
his face? It was almost like he was taunting me.
I would end up staying up most nights because I
was scared to fall asleep.

That damn alarm clock was steadily going off,
but I reached over and turned it off. I just laid my

head on the pillow, and it was already going off. I needed a damn day off, but today was not the day. Javon had court tomorrow, and I needed to go over some last-minute details about his case.

Five minutes later, I dragged myself out of the bed. I looked at the time. Damn, the kids. I ran to their rooms, but they were gone. I panicked. I ran to my room and grabbed my phone to call Nyesha.

"Hey, Mama."

"Hey, baby. Where are you?"

"I'm in school, Mama. Is something wrong?"

"No, no, I just got up, and I didn't see you or your sister."

"I came in your room, but were you sleeping. I decided not to wake you up. I know you've been having difficulty sleeping."

"Okay, baby. Did you eat?"

"Mama, I'm twelve now. I can take care of myself, and yes, I ate, and Myesha ate."

"Okay, baby. I love you. See you later."

"All right, Mama. Love you too."

I knew that they were growing up, but I still felt the need to make sure they were well taken care of. My girls were my life, even though Myesha's ass was difficult to deal with lately. My love for her had not changed. I would have to love her from a distance.

***

After battling Richmond's rush-hour traffic, I finally made it into the office. I quickly parked and hurried inside. This was one of those days when I wished I didn't have to work.

"Good morning, Dana," I said and walked into my office. I didn't mean to be short with her this morning, but I was dead-ass tired.

Before I could even settle in my seat, I heard Dana knocking. "Yes, Dana. Come in," I said with slight irritation in my voice. I looked at her as she entered my office.

"Good morning. Damn, you all right?" she said as she walked over to the window and opened up the blinds.

"I'm just tired. I barely get any sleep at night," I confessed.

"To be honest, you look like hell. How long has this been going on?"

"Ever since Trent's death. I just can't sleep. I just think I'm burned out."

"I'm worried about you. You seem more than tired. You're fatigued, and you look thinner, like you're not eating also. Trent is gone, but you need to take care of you because the girls need you."

"I know, but I am the only one they have right now, and I can't lie down and die."

"Ain't nobody saying that you need to lie down and die. Malaya, you have money; you don't need to work as hard as you do. You can take a week or so off. This office will still be here when you get back."

"I know. I just have this case, and he is counting on me so much. I can't let him down. His freedom is on the line."

"I understand all that, but Malaya won't be of any help to anyone if she is not healthy mentally and physically. I have a doctor friend; I want you to go see her. She can help you with what you're dealing with."

"I hope she ain't no damn shrink. I don't need anybody trying to analyze me." I shot her a dirty look.

"I'm about to get the number. You need to call her and set up an appointment." She walked out of the office.

Maybe she was right. I didn't tell her the full story because it wasn't her business. I did need something to help me sleep. I felt like if I continued like this, I was going to lose my sanity.

I made an appointment to see the psychiatrist the next afternoon. Maybe she could prescribe something that could calm my nerves and put me to sleep at night.

After talking to the doctor and letting her know what I was going through, she prescribed a low dosage of Ambien, which would help me sleep at night. I was happy because I felt like a zombie walking around.

Javon

The last few days were spent in a daze. It was like the world was closing in on me. I had no one to turn to and nowhere to hide. All the good I did for motherfuckers, you'd think they'd remember it, but they didn't. I was alone. Tania was too busy worrying about the next bitch; and Malaya, shit, she was too worried that the police might be watching us, so she didn't want to meet up unless it was at the office. I felt like that bitch used me to kill her husband, and now she was acting brand new.

I sipped some more of my Cîroc and took a few more drags of my weed. I sat back on the steps of this abandoned building. I usually came here when I wanted to clear my mind. I really thought this shit was going to disappear, but the closer I got to the court date, reality set in. I was also hurting for my little niggas, Li'l Trigger and Sword Man. Them niggas were nothing but twenty and twenty-one. I ain't goin' to lie; they were young as fuck. Now that I looked back, I should've never let them join the crew. All the regrets and what-ifs didn't matter because it was too late for all that.

I peeped a dark Suburban truck inching toward where I was sitting. At first, I didn't think anything of it, but the closer the vehicle got, the more something appeared to be wrong. I saw the back window slowly going down. I reached for my Glock, but it was too late.

Brap! Brap! Brap! I got hit in my chest. I got up and ran to the side, trying to fire back. They sped off down the street. I started to feel hot, and I was dizzy. I touched my chest and noticed blood was everywhere. I was losing consciousness, but I was determined not to die.

I reached in my pocket and pulled out my phone. I thought about calling 911 but, fuck, I had my gun with me. I took a quick glance around, and I barely wiped the gun with my shirt. I saw a little hole by the side of the building. I stuck the gun down in there. Blood was everywhere, and I was weak as fuck. I dialed 911.

"911, how may I help you?"

"I've been shot. I'm at 602 North Thirty-second Street."

"What's your name, sir?"

"Javon Sanders," I said before I collapsed to the ground.

Malaya

Javon was supposed to meet up with me to discuss his case, but he never showed up. I called his phone numerous times, but it just rang out. This was so not like him. Even though we had our personal issues, he was always on point when it came down to handling business.

After numerous times of trying his number, I started to panic. His court date was tomorrow, so where was my client at? I sure hoped this boy didn't do anything stupid like run. Maybe it was nothing. I waited for another hour, and he still hadn't shown up. I sent out two texts to him.

"Dana, has Mr. Sanders canceled his appointment?"

"Not that I know of. I thought you talked to him, since he is bae." She giggled.

"Girl, you are a mess but, no, I haven't spoken to him. I'm worried; this is so not like him."

"I'm sure he's just tied up, handling business. He will call soon."

"I hope so," I said and walked back into my office.

I dialed the attorney who was representing one of his codefendants.

"Hello," Attorney Newton answered.

"Hello, this is Mrs. Ipswich. My client, Javon Sanders, and your client, Anthony Biggins, are codefendants."

He cut me off. "Yes, Mrs. Ipswich. How may I help you?"

"I was wondering if everything was okay with your client. I had an appointment with my client, but I can't reach him."

"Everything is fine with my client. He is ready to plead guilty."

That shit caught me off guard. This was my first time hearing that he pled out. That was strange. I wondered, what did he plead to, and what deal did the state offer him?

"Okay, thanks. Sorry to bother you." I hung up before he could respond.

I was bothered as hell. I tried to tell Javon that he should've taken a plea. But he was so caught up on how real he was. I swear his ass was gonna find out that these niggas ain't loyal, and when it comes down to it, it was every man for himself.

I looked at the time; it was a little after eleven a.m. I wasn't going to sit around waiting any longer. He knew where to find me. I knew one thing; his ass better call me before it was too late.

I cleaned up my desk, closed my computer, grabbed my briefcase, and locked my office.

"Well, I'm leaving early today. Mr. Sanders still didn't show or call me, so I'm going home. He has court in the morning, so I'm hoping he will show up sometime soon."

"Okay, lady, take care, and please get some rest. I'm going to send out some e-mails and do some work."

I really missed living in a huge house. This house was okay but not like the other house. I couldn't wait to really buy another big house. I took my clothes off, and I put on my sweats and a T-shirt. I cut the television on; I loved watching the midday news news. There were a few minor crimes and a terrible accident. I picked up my phone; I was about to send out another text when something on the television caught my attention.

"Yes, the victim is Javon Sanders. He was shot multiple times last night on the six hundred block of Thirty-second Street. If I can, I'll give you a background on the victim. A few months ago, we did a report on him when he was arrested and charged with multiple counts of robbery, drug charges, and multiple murders. He was out on bond and was believed to be in court tomorrow to answer to these charges. The police are asking that if anyone has any information pertaining to this shooting, please contact the Richmond Police Department."

I dropped the phone. Javon was shot last night, and I didn't know about it. That's when it hit me; I didn't really know anything about this man. I'd never been to his house, and I'd never met his family. I quickly let those thoughts out of my mind. I needed to know what hospital he was in. I picked up the phone and started calling around. I was on the last one when the receptionist told me that she couldn't give out any info on the phone. That kind of let me know that he was there. I grabbed my purse and my car keys and ran out of the house.

My mind was racing. Even though we went through so much, I still didn't want anything to happen to him. The news didn't say how serious he was, but I knew that if he was in the ICU, it couldn't be anything good. I was feeling guilty for the way I treated him. "God, please let him make it," I begged God.

After sitting there for a few, I decided to go to the hospital. I was his attorney, and I needed to know if he was going to be all right. I pulled into the hospital parking lot and quickly parked. I then got out and ran up the stairs. I didn't have any time to sit there and wait for no damn elevator. By the time I got to the front desk, I was out of breath. "Hello, my name is Malaya Ipswich, and I'm here to visit Javon Sanders."

"Hello. Hold on a second." She went back to looking at her computer screen. "Can I please see your ID? Mr. Sanders is under police security, and I have to make sure you provide proper identification."

I reached into my purse to retrieve my driver's license. I handed it to her. I wished she would hurry the fuck up. I was eagerly waiting to see him. She finally handed my driver's license back to me and then told me the room number. I took off running toward the escalator, my heart pumping fast. I was feeling all sorts of emotion. Part of me was hoping he was all right, and the other part, well, let's just say it wasn't good thoughts.

I walked up to the guard and showed him my ID. He glanced at my name and gave me the okay to enter the room. I walked in as the nurse was walking out. "Hello. How is he?"

"Are you a close relative or friend?" She looked me up and down.

"No, I'm his attorney." I walked off on her.

I looked at him lying in the bed. He didn't look like himself. He was hooked up to a machine. I stepped closer to him; his face was black, and he was swollen. "Hey," I said. He was sleeping, so he couldn't hear me. I kind of felt a little bit of pity for him because we were fucking. I stood there for another ten minutes, just making small talk. It was obvious that he wasn't going to wake up.

A different nurse entered the room. "Hello, there. Your friend is one lucky fella. He is in a medically induced coma. The doctors are trying to reduce the swelling in his brain. The next few days will be very critical."

"Wow. How many times did he get shot?"

"I believe it was three times. That's why I say he was a lucky one. I can't begin to tell you how many others come in here with his kind of injuries, and I don't have to tell you the rest. He's a fighter, though," she said before she checked his vitals and exited the room.

I stayed a few minutes later, and then I decided to leave. I gave him a kiss on the cheek, but by the time I lifted my head up, drama kicked off.

"So, you just had to show your face up in here, huh?" this little ghetto bitch said while popping gum.

"Excuse me? I don't think it's a crime for me to visit my client who, by the way, has court tomorrow morning."

"Bitch, just 'cause you've got on a motherfucking suit doesn't make you any more special than the rest of us bitches. You think I'm stupid; I know yo' ass been fucking my baby daddy. But you know what, bitch? He ain't goin' to leave me; trust that. You were just a piece of pussy to him. He loves his children and me. You're an old-ass bitch anyways. My daddy doesn't want that ol' wrinkled-ass pussy."

"Listen, little bitch, I didn't even want my no-good-ass husband, so why in this world would you think I want a nigga with a bunch of bebe kids and a ghetto-ass baby mama? Little girl, I'm only interested in those dollars he's paying me to defend him. You can have the dick. Trust me, it wasn't all that anyway." I winked at that ho before I walked out of the room.

That bitch just bothered my fucking nerves with that bullshit. See, these younger bitches didn't know when to shut up. I pressed the button and waited for the elevator to come up. I shouldn't have let that bitch get me all riled up, but she was out of place. How dare she try to check me over a nigga who was sniffing up my behind like a sick puppy? Wrinkled pussy? That bitch had no idea how her baby daddy loved burying his head deep into this pussy. "Ha-ha, silly bitch." I burst out laughing.

I got on the elevator and took out my phone. I needed to let the courts know that he was in the hospital and would be there for a while. I needed to also get a copy of the police report so that I could use it as a possible defense when his trial came up.

I stopped by the court clerk's office to give them an update of what happened. His court date was postponed immediately. The clerk told me that I'd get a notice with a new date. I decided to head home. It had been a long day, and I could use a relaxing bath and a glass of wine.

I pulled up to the house and was about to pull into the driveway when I noticed an unfamiliar car parked by the side of the street. I looked but didn't see anyone sitting inside. I pulled into my driveway, and then I noticed the two detectives standing at my door. I parked and jumped out. "How may I help you?" I said in a very serious tone.

"Hello again, Mrs. Ipswich. How are you doing?"

"I'm doing quite fine. I thought I told your ass last time to contact my lawyer if you had any more questions. Do I need to pay a visit to your supervisor? 'Cause I damn sure will," I stated.

"You know, Mrs. Ipswich, for the life of me, I can't figure out why a woman who claims she was so in love with her husband, as you claimed, would not want to find his killer."

"You know nothing about me. You're fishing around because you're too damn lazy to go out

there and find the real killer or killers. I loved
my husband despite our differences. Maybe you
need to go and check that faggot he was sleeping
with. My husband broke it off with him to work
on our marriage."

"Or I can go and talk to that client of yours.
What's his name? Javon Sanders. Tell me, Mrs.
Ipswich, did your husband know that you were
fooling around on him with your client?"

"Get off my fucking property, and I will be
down at the office in the morning filing a harassment charge against you." I quickly opened my
door and stormed inside, leaving them standing
out there.

I flopped down on the couch and threw my
briefcase on the floor. That bastard caught me
off guard when he mentioned Javon's name. Out
of all the clients I represented, why would he
single him out? My investigative instinct was in
full mode. I kicked my heels off and walked into
the kitchen. I needed a strong drink to calm my
nerves. These damn kids were going to have to
fend for themselves tonight because I was going
to lie down. I needed to figure out this shit.

I took a quick shower and got into bed. I tried
to fall asleep, but I couldn't. That detective's
voice kept echoing in my head. I had no idea

what was going on but, whatever it was, I didn't want to have any part of it.

The next morning, I was up bright and early. I was still tired because I didn't get any sleep the night before. I was nervous because I know that Javon killed Trent, and I wasn't sure that the police weren't on to him. At first, I trusted Javon because, in my mind, he was a real street nigga, and I really thought that he would not fold. Over the course of time, however, I didn't know if I really could trust him. I was an attorney, and I'd seen too often where the hardest niggas folded under pressure. There was no way I was going down with this nigga for anything concerning Trent. I worked too hard to fucking lose everything.

I got into the office at a quarter to ten. Dana was on the phone, so I waved and walked into my office. I dialed Isiah's extension. "Hey, are you busy?"

"No, what's going on?"

"I need to talk to you about a possible case."

"Okay, I'll be over there in a sec."

I hung up the phone and leaned back into my recliner. I hated to bring my partner into my personal business, but I thought it was time. I really needed to get a great defense on my side, just in case these bitch-ass detectives wanted to play.

There was a loud knock at the door. "Come on in," I hollered.

Isiah's fine ass entered my office. Too bad his ass wasn't into my kind, and when I say my kind, I mean he was as gay as a baby. It was a damn shame because he was a fine-ass specimen of a man.

"What's up, babe?" he asked as he flopped down on my sofa.

I turned my chair around to face him. "I think I need to hire you."

"Hire me? For what?" he looked at me suspiciously.

"Well, ever since Trent got killed, these two detectives have been harassing me, showing up to the office and also to my home. I feel like they are accusing me of having something to do with his murder."

"Really? Girl, that's blasphemy. You couldn't hurt a fly if you wanted to." He giggled.

I wasn't in the mood to joke because something inside of me was telling me that there was a storm brewing. "I just want to hire you just in case anything pops off. I know you're one of the best out there, plus I know you have my best interests at heart."

"Well, you know you're the sister I've always wanted. I will talk to my friend down at the station to see if he's heard anything about an investigation. Okay, so since I'm now your attorney, is there anything you need me to know?"

"No, not at all. I was home with my husband when he was killed. I don't have any motive since we were going to counseling and working on our marriage. They damn sure can't say it was for his money because everybody knows that the money was mine."

"Okay, got you. You know how these police are desperate to close a case when one of their own is killed. Trent might've retired, but he will always be considered one of the boys in blue."

"Well, I have too much to worry about. I have to raise my girls now that Trent is gone. I need to find us a new house and get them situated again."

"Have you thought about taking a leave for a little while? You've been through a lot lately."

"I can't. I have this case that I'm preparing to take to trial. That's another thing; he got shot up, so he is in the hospital, fighting for his life. This case is starting to get so difficult."

"I can take it over for you. I mean, the judge knows you just lost your husband, so I don't see any objections."

"I know, but . . ." I massaged my temples. "I have to handle this one, but thanks for the offer."

We ended up talking for a little while longer, and then he went back to his office. I trusted that I was making the best decision because, next to me, Isiah was the best defense attorney.

I wished I could take him up on that offer to take a leave, but I knew Javon would have a fit, and I wasn't ready to deal with that.

I went over a few cases, answered some e-mails, and set up my calendar for the next month. I decided to leave early; I had a few errands to run.

"Hey, please send an invoice over to these clients," I said to Dana and handed her a folder.

"You going to lunch? I was going to join you."

"No, I'm leaving for the day. I have some business to take care of."

"Oh, okay."

Without responding, I smiled and walked off. I got in my car and headed to police headquarters. I needed to talk to Mr. DA himself. I parked my car and headed into the office.

"Hello. I'm here to see District Attorney Devon Williams."

"Your name please, and do you have an appointment?"

"My name is Attorney Ipswich and, no, I don't have an appointment."

"Well, he might be working on a case. Hold on; let me check."

That was all I wanted you to do, bitch, not tell me what the fuck you thought. I stood there, waiting patiently as she hung the phone up.

"The first door on the left."

I smiled at her old ass and walked off. I already knew where his office was located because I'd been in here numerous times. I didn't bother to knock. I pushed the door and entered the office.

"The beautiful Malaya." He stepped around the desk and gave me a tight hug, squeezing my ass. "Ass still firm," he whispered in my ear. He walked back to his huge mahogany desk and sat there, smiling from ear to ear.

"Hello, Devon. It's nice to see you." I crossed my legs and sat up straight.

"Hmm. So, what did I do to receive this visit from the beautiful defense attorney?"

"I want to talk off the record."

"All right, talk."

"I need a favor. I need you to drop the charges against my client."

He looked at me like he did not understand what I just said. After a few moments, he spoke. "What the hell are you talking about? What scum bag are you referring to now?"

"Javon Sanders."

"Ha-ha. Oh, him. You know I can't do that. The State of Virginia has been trying to get this bum and his crew off the streets for a decade. This is major, real major. Shit, we're all getting raises after this case is over."

"Devon, you are an asshole, you know that? A man's life is on the line, and you're worried about a fucking raise?"

"Come on, Malaya, stop being so uptight. I've thrown away a lot of cases before for you, but this one is out of the question. I'm just the messenger boy on this one. I take orders from my bosses, and if I lose, I will lose my job also."

"So, you're worried about this piece of shit job? You can start your own firm."

"Malaya, sorry to inform you, I'm not rich like you. I need this job to take care of my family."

"I understand. Well, I tell you what, I haven't had any dick in a while, and I miss sucking your dick, so how about we meet up Friday night for a little night rendezvous?" I licked my lips and smiled.

He sat there, thinking. "Well, yes, it would have to be after nine. The wife will be going out to her parents' house for the weekend."

"Deal. I'll call you on Friday." I got up and walked out of the office.

See, Mr. District Attorney and I go all the way back. We were both in law school, but he wanted more. He wanted to be a district attorney so, after a few years, he went back to finish his studies. It's kind of crazy because, right after he lost his first case to me, we ended up fucking, and after that, we would sneak off every chance we got. He was married, so it got kind of hectic, sneaking off without being seen. I finally had to break it off because his annoying-ass wife would blow him up all the damn time. The nigga's head would be in my pussy, and the phone would constantly be ringing, interrupting my nut.

After I left his office, I was more optimistic about Javon's case. Speaking of Javon, I decided to drop by the hospital and pay a quick visit. I just hoped that his deranged bitch was nowhere in sight. I swear, I hated a ghetto-ass, weave-wearing, gum-popping bitch with a loud mouth. Shit, I saw why he wanted a woman with class.

I circled the hospital parking lot for damn near fifteen minutes. I was getting frustrated and was about to leave. I spotted a car pulling out, so I immediately positioned myself to pull in. I saw another car trying to steal the space. I honked my horn and cut him off. "Fuck, you see me waiting," I yelled out of my window.

"Fuck you, bitch," he yelled back.

I didn't bother to respond. I parked and grabbed my purse. I was in an upbeat mood, so I pranced to the clerk's desk with my ID already in hand. "Hello. I'm here to see Javon Sanders, and here is my identification." I handed it to her.

She took it, looked at it, looked back at her screen, and then looked at me. "I'm sorry, ma'am, but you're not allowed to visit the patient."

"What? You're mistaken. I'm his attorney, and I just saw him yesterday." I was annoyed as fuck; this bitch was tripping.

"Ma'am, yes, but you are on the 'do not allow' list. I'm sorry about that, but until that is lifted, you cannot see the patient."

I noticed that there were people around, staring at me. I grabbed my ID and stormed off. That's when it hit me: that dumb-ass bitch must've put that shit on there. That ho was weak as hell for pulling that stunt.

I stormed out of the lobby and walked to my car. This little bitch had tried it. Seems I'ma have to show her little ass that, no matter what she does, her man is still going to fuck me and suck me. Young bitches kill my nerves, I thought before I pulled off.

CHAPTER NINE

Malaya

It was Friday, and I was in a great mood. Matter of fact, I was looking forward to seeing Mr. District Attorney himself, but I kind of love how I pronounced that. It kind of put a sexy edge on his name. I loved a man with power, and if you saw how he managed himself around the courtroom, you would definitely see what I was talking about.

I dropped the girls off at their grandmother's house. Even though that miserable bitch still tried to accuse me of having something to do with her son's murder, I still allowed them to go visit her. Plus, they were close with their cousins. I hurried home so I could take a shower. I had to make sure my pussy was well trimmed, douche it out, and wash it carefully with my Dove body wash. I welcomed the warm water beating down on my tired body. It had definitely been a rough week for me, so I was ready to relax and unwind.

I grabbed a pair of my Victoria's Secret sexy lace panties and bra. I lotioned down with my Laura Mercier Ambre Vanillé Body Butter. This cream was on the expensive side, but it was well worth it because it moisturized my skin and left my skin soft, just the way I liked it.

I called Devon's phone. "Meet me at the Marriott on Broad. I will let you know what room we're in." I knew I was being bold going to this hotel, because this was my regular spot with Javon. Oh, well. He was still in the hospital, so I was safe for now.

I set the alarm, grabbed my Michael Kors clutch, and walked out into the chilly night. I was looking forward to be in the company of this brown, tall, sexy brother. I sped away. I could've sworn I was being followed, but I brushed it off. I thought it was because the detectives ruffled my feathers.

I walked into the lobby of the Marriott and gave them my name. I paid, and the clerk handed me the keys. As soon as I got in the room, I pulled out my mini SecureGuard Six Power Outlet Tap spy camera. This was one of the latest from the spy shop. It was surprising how easy they made it to record things these days. I plugged it into the wall, beside our bed.

I dialed his number. "Where are you?"

"Pulling up to the hotel. What room are you in?"

"I'm in room 221."

"See you in a minute, and you better be butt-ass naked, waiting on daddy." He chuckled.

"You know it." I chuckled back at him.

I jumped out of the bed and stripped out of my clothes, keeping on my panties and my bra. Before I could jump back into the bed, I heard a tap on the door. I walked over, looked through the peephole, and then opened the door.

It was really refreshing to see him in casual clothes. He had on Nike sweatpants that were revealing his dick print. "Hey, babe," he said as he pulled me toward him and kissed me. I didn't resist. Instead, I started kissing him back.

"Damn, you all right? You're acting like you're starving for this pussy," I teased.

"Malaya, you know how much I love this pussy." He grabbed my crotch, pulling the panties down. We made it to the bed, and he let me go and hurriedly removed his clothes. His dick was already hard, and my pussy was soaking wet. I hadn't had any dick since the last time Javon and I fucked. Plus, getting new dick was always better. I was careful to turn my back to the video, but his performance was on center stage. He sucked on my clit and licked my ass from front to back. His head was buried deep between my legs. "Oweii, baby, I missed this. Don't you hold this pussy from me anymore," he gasped as he dug back in.

I wrapped my legs around his neck while I slowly ground on his face. My body tensed up as my heart rate sped up. I gripped his head and shoved it all the way in. My muscles tightened as my legs trembled. Juice spilled out onto his face. He sucked harder, using his tongue to clean up the spilled juice.

My pussy was throbbing hard, and my insides were tingling. I wanted to feel this hard, pretty dick all the way inside of me. "Come on, babe. Let me feel you inside of me." I pulled him up toward me and widened my legs. He got up and reached for his pants, pulling out a pack of Magnum condoms. He opened the pack and placed one on his dick. He then lifted my legs and eased into me slowly. "Aw, aw, aw," I moaned as I put my arms around his back. He looked into my eyes with his dark bedroom eyes and slowly fucked me. This man was definitely experienced and knew all of the ways to touch a woman's insides. He was satisfying me in a way that made me wish that I could savor the moment. I had to break my stare. There was no way I could allow myself to fall for this man. I was here for one reason and one reason only.

I threw the pussy on him, slowly grinding on his dick in a way that turned him on more. He gripped my waist and pulled me up to him. I felt his dick all the way in my stomach. The pressure was intense but not enough to make me back down. Each stroke he threw, I matched it. My pussy muscles tightened around his shaft. I gripped my nails into his skin, but that quickly made him slow down.

"Don't leave no marks, babe."

I smiled at him and eased my fingers off him. He quickly dove back into what he was doing before. The veins in my head were enlarged as I used everything in me to stop from screaming. I braced myself as I came all over him. That only made him dig deeper inside of me. I braced myself against the headboard as he broke my walls down. His veins were enlarged, and his strokes were longer.

"Aarghhhhhhh," he screamed out. I held him tight as I exploded also. He lay on top of me, quiet. After a few minutes, he got up. "That was some good shit right there," he said as he walked off into the bathroom. I was tempted to check the video, but I was too scared that he might catch me. I lay on my back, just thinking about how pleasurable that was.

"Hey, you ain't fall asleep on me, did you?" He chuckled as he picked up his cell phone and checked it.

Matter of fact, he was correct. It was as if someone sucked the energy out of me. I'd waited on him until I dozed off. "You took too long in there." I sat up in the bed. I wanted to go to the bathroom, but I was worried he might become suspicious of the plug into the wall. "You want to order something to eat?"

"No, I have to get going. I thought Priscilla was going to be at the cabin with her parents, but she just texted me saying she was on the way home."

"Oh, okay, that's fine. I so wish I could have had you all night," I pretended like I was disappointed.

"Cheer up, babes. You know I'm only with her because of her father's connections."

I wanted to burst out laughing because this fool actually thought I gave two fucks about him and the senator's daughter. That's right, Mr. District Attorney was married to Senator Muir's daughter. That was one of the reasons why he was so careful not to be caught up in any kind of drama. Because that would definitely bring shame on the senator and his daughter.

We chatted for a few, and then he got dressed. "It was nice to see you again, Malaya." He gave me a hug.

"It was definitely my pleasure, Devon." I hugged him back. "So, you're sure you can't drop the case against my client?"

"Malaya, don't turn this into an argument. I've already told you I can't do that. Not on this case, but you can call me on your other cases." His phone started buzzing. "I've got to run. Thanks for a great time, babe," he said and went out the door.

I ran to the door and locked it. I was tired, and my pussy was sore from all the fucking we did. I was ecstatic because this time was more business than pleasure. I walked over to the wall and pulled out the camera. "Let's see if you still feel this way," I said to myself.

I decided to take a shower, and then I ordered room service. I was exhausted, so I decided to spend the night. After all, I paid for the entire night. I ordered steak, well done, with mashed potatoes. I also ordered a bottle of expensive wine. The price wasn't cheap, but I had money, so I wasn't worried. I checked my e-mail as I waited on my food.

I heard my phone ringing, so I grabbed it. It was Nyesha calling. "Hey, baby girl."

"Mama, where are you? Can you come and get me?" she asked.

I knew my child, and I know something wasn't right. "Nyesha, what's wrong, baby?"

"Mama, Grandma over here talking 'bout how you killed Daddy off. I told her to stop talking 'bout you like that, and she's talking 'bout I'ma be worthless just like you."

"Say what?" I jumped off the bed and grabbed my clothes off the sofa. Before she could respond,

I was dressed, minus my underwear, 'cause I had no idea where they were, and God knows I didn't have time to find them.

"Please come and get me, Mama, before I snap on this lady."

"Where is your damn sister at?"

"Sitting in there with her."

"I'm on my way." I hung up the phone before she was able to say a word.

I grabbed the videotape, put it into my purse, took a long, good look around the room, and left. I practically ran to the elevator. I was mad as fuck, and only God knew what I might do to this bitch once I got there. See, I didn't care what a bitch said to me, but my fucking kids were off-limits.

I jumped in my car, and I was probably doing damn near ninety in a sixty-five mile-per-hour zone. I was trying my best to calm down, but the more I thought about what this bitch said to my child, the more my blood pressure rose. A ride that was supposed to take me about twenty-five minutes took me less than twenty minutes. I parked my car and ran up to the doorway. I banged as hard as I could on the door.

"Who the hell is that beating on my door like that?" I heard that ol' hog say as she opened the door.

"Where is my child at?" I pushed past her.

"I'm right here, Ma," Nyesha said as she walked over to me.

"Get your shit, and get your sister, and y'all go into the car. I'll be out there in a minute."

"Ma, let's just go." She grabbed my hand.

"Let me go! And do what I tell you to do."

"You're not welcome up in my house. My son's blood is on your hands."

I watched as my daughter gathered her shit and called her sister. She pranced downstairs with her face balled up. I didn't give a fuck about her and her attitude right now. As soon as the girls walked out the door, I dug into that old bitch's ass.

"Let me tell you something, you old hog. Don't ever talk to my fucking daughter the way you talked to her today. Bitch, if you have a fucking problem with me, address me, bitch."

"You low-class whore. I told my son you weren't worth shit, but his ass didn't listen. You killed him; you are a murderer! I will be there when they arrest you, and I'll be there when they stick that needle in your arm."

"Ha-ha, you're a funny old bitch. I'm done arguing with you. Like I said, the next time you address my child, I'm gonna knock yo' fucking head off. Mark my words."

"Get out of my house! Get out!" she screamed.

"Bitch, why are you worried about me? You should be worried about that faggot your son was fucking."

"I rebuke you in the name of Jesus. My Trent was not gay. You are trying to drag his name in the mud so you can cover up your dirt, you evil . . ."

I looked at that bitch, turned away, and walked out before she could finish her sentence. I walked to my car and got in. I started the car, reversed, and pulled off.

"Ma, I didn't want to leave. Why did I have to go? That was her and Nyesha arguing."

"Shut the hell up, little girl. Where the hell were you when all of this was going on? You act like that ain't your twin; that is the closest person to you. If somebody jumps out there with her, you should be the first one to protect her. That old woman had no right to say the shit she said to your sister," I lashed out.

I didn't want to hear shit else right now, so I cut up the music. My day started off good but, thanks to that old bitch, I was ending it in a fucked-up way.

As soon as I got in the door, I poured a glass of wine and walked upstairs. This was one fuck that I could say was well worth it. Before you knew it, I was dozing off. I was tired, mentally and physically.

CHAPTER TEN

Javon

These motherfucking niggas almost took my life. On my seeds, I swore I was gonna kill everyone who had something to do with it. The doctors told me I was lucky; I didn't think it was luck. I thought it was more like the Big Bro Upstairs was looking out for me. I knew it was a long road to recovery, but I was ready 'cause I had shit to handle out in these streets.

I was daydreaming until I heard someone enter the hospital room. I opened my eyes, and I noticed it was Tania. "Hey, babe," I said as she walked in with a plate in her hand.

"Hey," she said dryly.

"You a'ight?"

"I'm good." She sat down in the chair.

I had no idea what her ass was sulking about. To be honest, I was in too much pain to really give a fuck.

"Yo, so you were fucking that lawyer bitch, huh?"

"Damn, B, a nigga's fighting for his life, and here you are, coming at me with some shit that's not true."

"I talked to your doctor; you're doing much better. I done waited long enough. I saw your fucking text messages between you and that ho. How could you do this to me and your kids?"

"Where the fuck is my phone, and how did you get it?"

"You're a fucking asshole. I just find out you're cheating, and you're worried about your fucking phone. I swear to God, I fucking hate your ass right now. How could you? I gave up my life to help you. You think I'ma let this bitch just walk in and fuck up what we have? Over my dead fucking body. You hear me?" she screamed.

I tried to sit up in the bed, but the pain was unbearable. This bitch knew she wouldn't be doing all this screaming if I wasn't in this bed. I'd never put my hands on my children's mother, but I definitely would bounce on that ass ASAP.

"Yo, B, cut all this drama. I ain't trying to hear that shit right now. I'm with you, so I don't know why you're tripping like that."

"You think that's enough because you're with me? There were days when I called you, and you didn't pick up your phone, and you lied that you were out grinding. Nah, you were out screwing this bitch."

"Yo, you need to go home. My body is hurting, and I want to go to sleep."

"Yeah, right, nigga. You keep playing with me, and I'ma show you and that bitch I ain't nothing to play with."

I pressed the call button.

"Yes, may I help you?"

"Can you please come in here and escort Miss Davis out of here?"

"I'll be in there in five minutes."

"You're dirty as fuck. You goin' to call the fucking people on me? I'll just fucking leave. You ain't got to worry 'bout me coming back up here. Now your bitch can come. Oops, I forgot, her ass can't." She threw my phone at me, grabbed her things, and left, still cursing.

"Fuck," I yelled out. I felt a sharp pain in my back. I knew I had to be careful. The doctor said that if one of the bullets had gone in one inch farther, it would've hit my spinal cord, and I would be crippled. I swear, I ain't no spiritual nigga, but a nigga definitely appreciated the love.

As soon as I was sure that she was gone and not playing her little games, I grabbed my phone and scrolled through it. I thought the police had my phone. I wondered how the hell she got it. I decided not to use this phone anymore. The shit might be tapped. I didn't see them just letting it go, just like that.

I used all my might and reached for the hospital phone. I dialed Malaya's number.

"Hello," her sexy voice echoed.

"Damn, you just left a nigga for dead, huh?"

"Who is this?"

"Damn! I ain't been gone that long, and you've already forgotten a nigga," I said jokingly, but I was so serious.

"Hello, Javon. I didn't expect to hear from you. How are you doing?"

"Damn, you put the professional voice on a nigga. Lemme find out you're around another nigga and shit. How come you ain't been up here to see a nigga and shit?"

"Really? Don't you call me checking me about shit. I came up there, and you had me on the 'no visitation' list."

"What? What are you talking about? I 'ont know nothing about that. Man, my stupid-ass baby mama must've done that shit. I ain't know nothing about it."

"Yeah, I met her the day I came to visit you. Her ass was carrying on, talking 'bout how you and I were screwing around. I swear, if I wasn't scared of getting locked up and messing up my law license, I would've beat her ass right in your hospital room."

Yeah, yeah, yeah. I wasn't trying to hear that shit. I didn't give a fuck how much Tania got on my nerves; there was no way I was going to sit back and watch anybody, and I mean anybody, beat her ass. Well, Malaya didn't know that, and there was no need for her to know that.

"Well, babe, I told you before, you ain't got nothing to worry about. I'm about to hit these nurses up and get your name taken off that list. I want to see you, babe. I was hoping you would be here once I opened my eyes."

"Hmm. Whatever, Javon. I will be up there tomorrow to discuss your case."

"Malaya, I love you, girl."

All I heard was the dial tone in my ears. Damn, I can't get none of these bitches to cooperate with a nigga. I bet you if I were dead, their asses would be all over me, crying and shit, talking about how good of a nigga I was. I ain't tripping. As soon as I get out of here, I am going to give them this dick. That was what they really wanted, to feel me all up in their guts.

I pressed my morphine button because the pain was killing me, plus I needed something to help me feel better. I felt helpless being up in this hospital bed without my gun. I started to feel the effects of the drugs and, before you knew it, I was dozing off.

At 4:00 a.m., the nurse entered the room to check my vitals. I was mad as fuck 'cause this bitch cut on the light, which woke me up. I wished her ass would just disappear. "Ay, what time the doctors come in? I'm ready to get out of here."

"Dr. Patterson will be in at nine a.m. He will be coming to see you."

"A'ight, cool." I closed my eyes, trying to doze off again. Hopefully, this bitch could keep her ass out of the room.

The next morning, I was up bright and early. I was ready to see what kind of news the doctors had for me. I wasn't feeling my best, but I was ready to get up out of here. Plus, a nigga ain't got no insurance, so I wasn't prepared to lie up in here so this motherfucking hospital could milk me dry.

I heard someone enter the room, so I figured it was the doctor. Instead, it was two dudes with shades on who were dressed in suits. I quickly recognized that they were no doctors but more likely law enforcement. I didn't say anything because, truthfully, I ain't got shit to say. I already told them pigs that I didn't see who shot me, and even if I did, I wouldn't tell them.

"Good morning, Mr. Sanders. My name is Detective Pelluso, and this is my partner, Detective Rosales."

"What's good?" I barely uttered.

"How are you feeling? I see you're doing much better than the last time we stopped by. We were under the impression that you may not make it," said Rosales.

"Oh, yeah, well, that's how it is sometimes. So, what's good? Do I need to call my lawyer?"

"No, we're here to chat with you. No lawyer is needed. Right, Pelluso?" He turned to his partner.

I had no idea what these niggas wanted with me but, whatever the fuck it was, I wasn't about to entertain it in any form.

"Mr. Sanders, how well do you know Mrs. Ipswich?"

"What do you mean?"

"Just what I asked. How well do you know Mrs. Ipswich?"

"She's my lawyer, but you already know that, right?" I asked sarcastically. I wasn't sure where this nigga was going with his questions, but I was feeling uneasy.

"Yes, we are aware that she is your lawyer. Let me come straight out and ask you a question. Are you and she involved on a personal level?"

"Nah, what gave you that assumption?" I grinned nervously. I had no idea what this fuck nigga was implying.

"Hmm. That's strange because we got word that you and Mrs. Ipswich have more than a client-lawyer relationship."

"Detective, I don't know where you're getting your info from, but she's my lawyer; that's all. But, anyway, what's all this questioning about? I'm pretty sure you didn't come here to check up on my relationship with my lawyer." I sat up straight.

"You're right. I have proof here that you and Mrs. Ipswich are more than friends." He placed some pictures in front of me. I grabbed the pics and looked down at them. They were pictures of Malaya and me when we first started fucking around.

"Where the fuck did you get these?"

"Mrs. Ipswich's deceased husband hired a PI who followed her around for quite a while. I believe he confronted her about her cheating, and that was why he was killed."

My throat tightened up on me. If this motherfucker was following her around, did he see when my B went up into the house? I calmed myself down. There was no way I was going to let them see me sweat, not even for a minute.

"You okay, Mr. Sanders? You're looking like you've got something you need to get off of your chest."

"Nah, I'm good. What I'm trying to understand is, if this is about Mrs. Ipswich and her husband, what the hell do you want with me?" I was ready for them to get the fuck out.

"Here is where you come in. We don't think Mrs. Ipswich killed Trent herself. We think she had help. We are coming to you to see if you would help us."

"Help you? What the fuck do you mean?"

"Help us build a case against her. We know you have that big drugs and weapons case coming up, so we're willing to make a deal if you help us out. Even if you had anything to do with the murder, I think I can talk to the DA, and he can give you full immunity. Trent was one of us, so solving his murder is really top priority right now."

"I 'ont know nothing 'bout no murder. I've got my own problems to worry about. Feel me?"

"Yes, we understand, and that's why we are here, trying to get you the best possible deal. Do you recall Mrs. Ipswich talking to you about her late husband?

"Nah, all we talked about was my case. I 'ont concern myself with other dudes."

"Mr. Sanders, Mrs. Ipswich is a very smart woman. Forgive me, but I have to be blunt. Don't let her sexy voice and a piece of pussy let you fall into her web of lies."

"I think it's time y'all get up out of here." I stared at both of them.

"Sure; here goes my card. Please don't wait too long because we're gonna get her, with or without your help, and if you're involved in any way, you will be going down also." He placed the card on the ice table. His partner nodded at me, and they exited the room.

What the fuck, yo? What has this bitch dragged me in? She never told me about no damn PI or the fact that he had pictures of us. If I knew that, my ass wouldn't have even killed that nigga. I ain't no fool; these niggas knew more than they were letting on. They didn't just choose me because I was fucking her.

I picked up the phone to call her, but I quickly decided not to. I needed to see where the fuck this was going. There was no way I was going to let this bitch drag me into her shit. I wasn't sure that her phone wasn't tapped. I decided to wait until she came up here today.

I couldn't sit still after they left. I was ready to get the fuck out of here. I felt like a sitting duck. I was pretty sure they were building a case against her, and I wanted no part of it. That bitch was goin' to have to take that by her damn self. As soon as I get out of here, I think it's time to find a new lawyer. Just in case her ass decides to put this shit on me. I didn't trust any of these bitches!

The doctor walked in my room after 2:00 p.m. We talked, and he asked me a few questions about how I was feeling. My lab results were back, and everything seemed perfect.

"So, Doc, how soon can I get out of here?"

"Well, Mr. Sanders, I think you're ready to be discharged Friday. We need to run some more tests to make sure you're ready."

"A'ight, that's cool."

He examined me, and then he left. I kind of felt what he was saying. I knew I was eager to leave, but I was still in a lot of pain. Today was Wednesday, so Friday wasn't too far. I lifted myself up and grabbed the card the detective left. I stared down at it until I tucked it under my pillow. I lay down, thinking all kind of things.

Malaya

I sat at my desk, going over some work. I was trying to see what angle I was trying to take with

Javon's case. As I swept through the mounting evidence they had against him, I realized that he was making a big mistake by going to court. I only wished his ass would have really listened to me. I was still reading when I heard a knock on the door.

"Come in," I hollered.

"I need to talk to you about the Javon Sanders case," Dana said with a concerned look plastered across her face.

"What? Did something happen that I don't know about?"

She sat down and crossed her legs. "Well, whatever I'm about to tell you is confidential. I mean, I want you to use it to prepare your defense but, please, you can't tell anyone, and I mean anyone, not even Javon," she said, sounding nervous.

"Dana, you've got my word. What is making you so nervous?"

"Well, I've been keeping it a secret because of his job, and he is married. I've been seeing the assistant DA for a while now. The other day, he was working while we went away for the weekend and, after a few drinks, he started talking about how they were gonna win the case against you. I didn't say a word, so he kept on talking. That's when he showed me a folder; it was the case that they had against Javon. To make a long story short, one of Javon's friends, who is supposed to be his closest confidant, turned state's evidence, and he is going to testify against him. They gave him full immunity."

"Really? Are you sure? If I can remember, Javon and Mann-Mann were like brothers." I shook my head in disbelief. I wasn't shocked; I knew how the game was played. I couldn't say I blamed him; I was just mad that my dumb-ass client couldn't see it coming.

"Yes. He asked me to promise him that I wouldn't say anything until you saw the witness list."

"You've got my word, but I need to call the DA's office and ask them for a copy of the witness list. That is the normal process, so no one will ever know you said anything."

"All right, boss. Got you." She smiled and got up.

"Dana, I appreciate you." I smiled at her.

After she walked out, I started to think. This nigga, Devon, knew about this, but he didn't say a word to me. See, this kind of made it easier for me to do what I was going to do. I saw everybody was out for self, so I was definitely only worried about me, myself, and I.

I heard a knock at the office door, interrupting my thoughts. I wondered what Dana wanted now.

"Come on in," I yelled.

As soon as the person entered, I realized it wasn't Dana. Instead, it was Detective Rosales and Detective Pelluso.

"What do you want? I told you to contact my lawyer if you needed anything," I said.

"This is a search warrant to confiscate your personal computer and papers," Rosales said while trying to hand me a piece of paper, but I walked off without taking it.

"You can't do that! I have confidential correspondence between my clients and me."

"I promise you, we're only interested in your personal conversations."

I didn't wait; I stormed out and grabbed the phone in the front office.

"Isiah, you need to get here ASAP! They are searching my office and confiscating my laptop. They can't fucking do this," I yelled in the phone.

"I'll be there in less than five minutes."

I hung up and walked to the window. I was furious as hell. These motherfuckers were not easing up. What the hell did they think they were going to find? Did they really think I was a stupid bitch? I mean, after all, I was a defense attorney. I did this shit for a living. I couldn't wait for this shit to be over; I was going to sue this fucking city for harassment.

In no time, Isiah's ass walked in and started going off about harassing his client. I swear, that man was a pit bull, and he knew the law.

"Your client is a person of interest in the murder of her husband. And this a search warrant signed by Judge Clarke." Rosales handed the paper to Isiah.

"Detective, no disrespect, but this is farfetched. My client is a very respectful member of the community, and she is a good-ass defense attorney. I think that alone should speak for the kind of person she is."

"Well, no disrespect, but I've seen cold-blooded killers who were preachers before. We are not going to stop gathering evidence until we got everything we need to charge someone with the murder of Detective Ipswich."

"My client has rights and, unless you're prepared to charge her with a crime, I will be filing a harassment charge against you and your office."

"Well, we are finished here for now, but I would love for your client and you to come see us down at the precinct. It's in her best interest if she cooperates with us from early on. You know the death penalty will be on the table for the brutal killing of a police officer."

"Good day, Detective," Isiah said and opened the main door, allowing them to walk out.

I pranced back into my office. I was mad as fuck. I hoped they'd hurry the fuck up with my laptop. I wasn't worried about them finding anything on there. I was angry because these detectives were like a pain in my ass that wouldn't leave. In front of people, I had to pretend like I didn't have any worries, but the truth was, deep down, I was shivering. Especially when that motherfucker mentioned the death penalty. A bitch like me wouldn't look good in no damn orange.

Isiah walked into my office and stood there like he was thinking. "I have no idea why they are so adamant about putting this murder on you. Malaya, please don't hold anything from me. I need to know everything so I can be prepared, just in case they decide to charge you."

"Isiah, you should know me better than that. I told you, I don't know who killed my husband, and I damn sure didn't kill him. They examined my hand for gunpowder residue the night of the murder, and there was nothing. I don't know what their fascination is with me or who is spreading lies about me, but I know I couldn't kill my children's father."

"Well, I'm going to start doing some investigating on my own. When you have time, send me all the names of anybody you think might've had a motive to kill Trent. Also, send me a copy of your financial statements. They need to come up with a motive and physical evidence before they can charge you. In the meantime, I suggest—and this is only a suggestion because this is your firm and I can't tell you how to run it—but I think you need to take a leave. Let me handle the Sanders case."

I sat there in silence, listening to what he was saying. I felt like I was drowning, and there was no way out. I doubted that Javon would agree to this, but I damn sure would ask him. I really needed a fucking break to get my thoughts in order. Only God, Javon, and I knew what really happened to Trent. I knew I wasn't talking, and God ain't say a word. As far as Javon . . .

"Thank you, but I need to talk with my client first, and I will let you know by tomorrow. Thank you, Isiah, for everything." I shot him a fake smile.

After he left, I put my head on my desk. I needed a second of quiet to get my head together. I must've dozed off because I got startled when Dana tapped me on my shoulder.

"Are you okay?"

"Yes, I'm fine." I quickly wiped my eyes.

She walked around to my chair and wrapped her arms around me. It was then that I started bawling. I had so much built up inside, I needed to let it out.

"Babe, I need you to know I've got you." She kissed me on my lips.

I was caught off guard. "What is you doing?" I stuttered.

"Malaya, I'm sorry. I just thought I would comfort you a little."

I removed her arm from around me, and I got up. I didn't know what she was thinking. I didn't knock gay people, but I didn't go that way. There's nothing another bitch could do for me.

"Listen, let's just forget that this happened. But please don't try me like that again. Don't you ever. You understand?"

"Yes. I'm so sorry, Malaya," she said and exited my office, hanging her head down in shame.

That was it for me. I was ready to get the fuck out of there. I turned my office computer off. I grabbed my briefcase and locked my office. I walked out to the elevator and pressed the button.

I got in my car, feeling depressed and distraught. I had no regrets that Trent was dead. Shit, if I had to do it all over again, I would. The way that bastard treated me, I swear he deserved every ounce of what he got. I just wished I had done it myself so I wouldn't worry about this nigga running his mouth.

Javon

It was early Friday morning, and I was too psyched to go home. I'd been in here for a minute, and I was ready to go. The block was missing me, and I was too eager to get back to my life. I grabbed my cell phone and called Tania. I totally forgot that I needed a ride out of here.

I dialed her number, and it rang out until her voicemail came on. I hung up and pressed redial. She picked up.

"What do you want?" she snapped.

"What the fuck you mean, what do I want?"

"Javon, I told yo' ass, it's over. You can go be wit' that lawyer bitch."

"Man, go ahead wit' all that. I've only got one woman, and that's you. Anyway, man, I'ma be discharged 'round eleven. I need you to come scoop me up and bring me some clothes and a pair of my sneakers."

"I already told yo' ass, I'm done with you. You carried the hell out of me. I bet you that bitch is laughing at me. You made a damn fool out of me, but I'm done. I'm taking my fucking kids and getting the fuck away from you."

"Tania, you better quit playing with me. You already know I will show the fuck off if you take my kids away. Yo, you better bring yo' ass up here at eleven to get a nigga." I hung the phone up on her bitch ass.

This bitch was gonna run me into another bitch's arms if she didn't tighten up on her attitude. I didn't know 'bout no other nigga, but I knew my black ass didn't want no bitch who was constantly complaining about me fucking another bitch. I mean, that's all I was doing was fucking, and in Malaya's case, I was using that bitch to beat this case. I planned on leaving that ho alone once this case was over. If Tania continued like this, her ass would be left also. I planned on leaving Richmond, and probably moving down to Florida with my big homie.

It was fifteen minutes to eleven. I dialed Tania's phone to make sure she was on the way, but the phone went straight to voicemail. I waited a few seconds, but it was still the same. I sat on the edge of the bed, dialing her number back to back. There was no response.

"Man, where the fuck you at? I told yo' ass eleven a.m. It's now eleven-fifteen. Where the fuck are you at? Call me back or something."

I sat there, feeling antsy. I checked my phone to see if I had any missed calls or texts. I knew there wasn't any because I was holding the phone in my hand. I thought about calling a cab, but I couldn't because a nigga was broke. I knew I had stacks on me when I got shot, but I had no idea what happened to them. Those police might've pocketed that shit. They were known for that.

At 2:00 p.m., the nurse walked in the room to inform me that they were going to clean up the room for another patient. In other words, the bitch was telling me that I needed to get the fuck out. I still had on the hospital gown, without boxers underneath, dick hanging and shit.

"Your ride is late; did you call?"

"Yeah, I did." I walked off.

"Let me get you another gown, so you can cover your backside." She shot me a strange look. Within seconds, she walked back into the room with a gown and some of those thick hospital socks.

"Good looking out."

"You're welcome."

I dialed Malaya's number.

"Hello," she answered.

"Yo, where you at?"

"Javon, what do you want?" she said with an attitude.

"Yo, I'm discharged, but I ain't got no ride up outta here."

"Did you call your bitch?"

"Man, chill out. You weren't worried about her before, so what is this all about now?"

"I'm not worried about you or that bitch. I was just wondering why she's not there to get you."

"Man, I 'ont know, but I need you to come scoop me up."

"All right." She hung up without saying anything else.

I wasn't stuttin' her. I just wanted to get out of here so I could get to my cars and my money. I never allowed a bitch to make or break me before, and I damn sure wasn't going to start now. I walked out of the room and walked toward the elevator.

"Mr. Sanders, you have to get in this wheelchair, so we can wheel you out of here. Stay right here while an aide grabs a chair."

I waited until she walked off, and then I got on the elevator. My side was still hurting bad, but it was nothing that I couldn't manage at the time. I got out of the elevator and walked outside. There was a bench nearby, so I walked slowly over and sat down.

I heard my phone ringing, so I answered it.

"Where are you?"

"I'm sitting by the emergency room entrance."

I saw when she drove into the parking lot. I got up so she could see me. She pulled up, and I walked to the car. I got in, put my seat belt on, and she pulled off.

"Man, I 'ppreciate it."

"No problem."

The ride was very quiet. Young Jeezy music was playing low. I wondered what the fuck was going on with her. "Yo, Malaya, what's going on with you, B?"

"Who said something was going on? You asked me to pick you up, and that's what I did."

"It's me you're talking to. Ever since I talked to you the other day, I feel like you've got some kind of attitude toward me and shit."

"Javon, maybe this was a mistake. Maybe we should have kept it on a professional level, because all this is too much."

"Man, now you're having regrets and shit. You wanted this just as much as I wanted this. Or was it that you were pretending that you wanted this?"

"Don't fucking turn things around. I should've never crossed the line with you. I had no idea you had a woman. I don't want to be in any kind of drama. I'm too old to be arguing with another woman over a damn man."

"You ain't got to argue with anyone. If I recall, I wanted us to move in and be a family, but you didn't want that! Even after the old nigga was gone, you still didn't want that. So that tells me that you ain't trying to see me as more than just your side nigga."

"Whatever you say! You think it looks good that my husband just passed and I'm already living with another nigga? Don't be foolish."

"Look good to who? This is our life; fuck e'erybody else."

"See, that's why you're a street nigga, and I'm the one with a degree, because you can't think with sense for once."

"What the fuck did you say? I ain't no dumb nigga. Man, let's just drop this shit."

I felt my anger coming on, so I decided to drop the subject. I knew the bitch was sneak dissing me, but I controlled myself. There was no reason to show out when I needed her to beat this case; or did I really need her? Hmm. I had the detective's number folded in my hand.

There ain't no pussy in my blood, but the more I thought about how this case might turn out, the more I was debating what I wanted to do.

"Where am I taking you to?" she asked, interrupting my thoughts.

"Take me to my crib."

I reluctantly gave her the address, but then why the fuck did I care? That bitch was too busy to get a nigga. Right now wasn't the right time to give a fuck about her feelings.

"So, umm, what's good wit' my case?"

"It's postponed because you got shot. I'm waiting to get a new date from the DA's office."

"Oh, okay, that's cool."

"Listen, Javon, I need to talk to you. There's a lot going on, and I really feel like I need to take a break—"

"A fucking break? What the fuck you mean? I'm in the fight of my life, and you're worried 'bout taking a break?" I yelled out, spit flying everywhere.

"Yes. I don't feel like this is a good time for me to provide the attention your case needs. I'm kind of sidetracked, dealing with some personal shit. My partner, Isiah at the firm, is very tenacious, and he can do just as good a job as I can."

"Nah, fuck that, B! I came to you; you accepted this case, so you will defend me. I'm not trusting my life with anyone outside of you! So, I suggest you get your personal shit together because you will defend me. Bitch, after everything I did for you? I blew that nigga's brains out for you. Did you forget that, huh? You fucking owe me," I yelled with everything in me.

"You better lower your fucking voice. I'm not that little bitch you're fucking with. I'm a grown-ass woman, and you don't tell me what the fuck to do."

"You have no idea who the fuck you're playing with! Don't think if you try to fuck me over that I would think twice about blowing your and your princesses' fucking brains out."

That bitch stopped the car in the middle of the street. "Let me tell you something, you little lowlife piece of shit, don't you ever threaten my fucking children. Fucking around with me will get you a life sentence in federal prison."

"Man, all you're doing is barking. You already know what it is."

She looked at me, rolled her eyes, and drove off erratically. I shouldn't have taken it there with her, but the way I was really feeling right now, I didn't have any more fucks to give. I was happy when she pulled on my street.

"Yo, you can let me out here."

She pulled over. I got out of the car without saying a word to her. Before I could hit the sidewalk, she pulled off, leaving the stench of burning tires.

I peeped that Tania's car was parked in the garage. That infuriated me more. This bitch was in the house, chilling, and I had to beg for a fucking ride. I didn't have my keys, so I banged on the door.

"Who is it?" she answered with an attitude.

"Yo, open the motherfucking door."

She did. I stepped past that bitch.

"Daddy is here," my baby girl screamed and jumped on me.

I cringed as her weight caused me to buckle a little. "Hey, baby girl." I grabbed her up even though the pain was unbearable.

My son then ran to me also.

"Y'all let Daddy sit down really quick."

"Daddy, I'm so happy you're home," Kymani said. This little man was the spitting image of me. He was my firstborn and the reason why I went so hard in these streets.

"Daddy, please don't leave us anymore," my daughter said as she squeezed me a little too tight.

"Baby girl, your daddy got you. Believe that!" I kissed the top of her head. I was so caught up with my kids that I didn't have any time to pay their mama any mind. I did notice that, when she walked past me, she shot me a dirty look.

After I played with them for a few, they ran off to go back to whatever they were doing. I got up and walked toward the bedroom. I closed the bedroom door because I knew it was going to get heated, and I didn't want my kids to hear any of it.

"Yo, why you ain't pick me up?"

"Boy, get out of my face! I told yo' ass, it's over. You must think I'm fucking playing, huh?"

"Really? That's how you goin' to carry a nigga when a nigga's down on his face?"

"Carry you? I've been there, booboo. I was the one who gave you money to get on your feet. I was the one who sat in the bathroom and washed your dirty drawers and your heavy-ass jeans because we were too broke to afford money to go to the Laundromat. I slept on the hard-ass floor with you when we only had one bed and the kids were on it. I was the one, Javon, not these other bitches. But who did you give your ass to kiss once you started making money? That's right. Me."

I stood there frozen as she spit out the times when we were struggling. I saw the tears flowing down her face, and her eyes said it all. I swear, I was a killer and I could deal with the streets, but Tania had my heart, and I hated to sit back and watch her hurt like this.

Over the years, I didn't think I was really doing any damage to our relationship because I busted my ass pulling all-nighters just so I could move them out of the hood. I did that. I bought her cars, made sure she had money to spend, but I spent less time with her.

I didn't know my parents because both of them motherfuckers were no good. My mother's mother raised me, and she did the best she could, which was almost nothing. Many days I went without food because she had to pay for rent, and the rest went to her medicine. That's when I turned to the streets, and the rest was history. I made a vow never to let my family go without, as long as I was breathing.

"Man, come here. Stop crying." I walked to her side of the bed and wrapped my arms around her.

"No, I don't want hugs. I don't want empty promises! I'm tired of all of this. You just going around, slinging your dick all over the place." She pushed me away.

"I'm not slingin' anything. Lemme talk to you real quick." I sat down beside her. Any other time, I would've thought that she was bullshitting, but not this time. I saw the seriousness in her face, and I knew she was done. I had to do something fast.

I tried to hold her hand, but she wasn't having that. I decided to stop forcing it. "Listen, boo. I know I fucked up. I know I put you through a lot of shit." I paused. I was trying to say the right shit, but I didn't want to sound like a bitch.

The sounds of gunshots interrupted my speech. I jumped to my feet to see where the fuck it was coming from, because it sounded too close for comfort. "Shhh. I think it's in here," I tried to tell her while I tiptoed to the closet to grab my gun I'd always kept in the closet. I didn't see it, so I turned around to ask her where she put my gun, but she was no longer in the room.

"I've got to get my babies! Noooo! My babies. Noooooooo!" I heard her screaming. I heard another round of gunshots. I opened the drawers; my gun wasn't there. I dug under the mattress and there it was. I grabbed it, checked for bullets, and ran out the door, busting. A masked gunman saw me, returned fire, and then ran out the door. My adrenaline was rushing as I chased after him, busting my gun. I was too late, though; he jumped into a dark Suburban truck similar to the one that pulled up the night I was shot.

I stood there. That's when it hit me that I needed to go check on my family! I saw Tania on the floor. I ran to her, but my legs would barely carry me. I fell down to my knees as I witnessed my bitch shot on the ground. I got up, turned around, and yelled for my children. "Jayel and Kymani." I ran into their rooms, yelling as my heart dropped. Their lifeless, gunshot-riddled bodies were sprawled across the bed. I collapsed on top of them.

"Aargggggggggggggggggghhhhhhhhhhhhhhh. Aarghhhhhhhhhhhhhh." I touched my little man's body, but I could tell he wasn't breathing. I then touched my daughter, and she was also gone.

I lay there, holding them close. I was afraid to move. I can't leave them alone. I just can't!

Malaya

When someone shows you who they are the first time, it's best you believe them. This wasn't the first time this nigga showed me his weak side, but he definitely grabbed my attention earlier when I was driving him home. I heard the weakness in his voice as he called himself threatening my girls and me. I didn't take it lightly at all.

I was happy when I dropped him off because I needed time to myself. He was a weak link that I needed to go away for good. There's no way I was going to let him keep holding me hostage. He never actually came out and said it, but I knew that he was referring to Trent's death. Some people said, "Pressure bursts pipes," and he was one pipe I believed was going to burst real soon. I had to figure something out and very soon.

I remembered when I first met him. He made my insides shiver, and whenever we made love, I got the best feeling ever. His dick was good, but I was so over that. I knew we could never be because he wasn't honest at first; plus, his ass was a ticking time bomb, ready to go off. I had to cut him loose after this case was over with because he had become a liability, and I couldn't risk him bringing me down with him.

After dinner, I decide to take a long shower. I rubbed my hand across my breasts as the water poured down on my body. I wished I had a man to massage the kinks out of them. I inserted my finger inside of me as I envisioned getting fucked. I ground harder as I climaxed. Pussy juice ran down my legs. I used my finger to wipe it up and then licked it off. Who needs a man when I can fuck myself? I got out of the tub and dried myself off.

I was just about to rub lotion over my body when my cell phone started ringing. Whoever that was needed to wait, but I guessed that wasn't an option because the phone continued ringing nonstop! I grabbed the phone off the bed. I noticed it was Mr. District Attorney himself. I smiled. Let me find out he wanted some of this good pussy.

"Hello," I answered in my sexy voice.

"Malaya, where have you been? There has been a murder at your client Javon Sanders's house."

"What the hell are you talking about? I just dropped him off at home about two hours ago!"

"It's the worst murder scene I've ever seen. His children and his girlfriend are dead. It's a massacre in here."

"Is he alive?"

"Yes. He is being questioned by our detectives. I think you should get down here ASAP."

"Stop the questioning until I get there," I demanded.

I hung up the phone and took a seat on the bed. I kind of wanted this to turn out a different way. I would've felt much better if I'd gotten the call that he was dead. Yes, I knew it sounded cold but, shit, at least I wouldn't have to worry 'bout him running his mouth about Trent's death!

I let out a long sigh. I might as well get dressed and go down there to see what kind of shit he done gotten his ass into now. I threw on some sweatpants, a top, and a pair of sneakers. I grabbed my cell phone and headed out the door.

When I pulled up at the address that I dropped him off at, police cars were everywhere. I pulled to the side of someone else's driveway and parked. "Ma'am, you can't go through there. This is a crime scene," a uniformed officer said to me.

"She's cleared," Devon said.

I walked underneath the crime tape. "What the hell happened here?" I put my hand akimbo.

"Your client is over there."

"All right, thanks."

I walked up the steps of the two-story brick house. I took a deep breath and walked over to where Javon was sitting down with his head buried in his lap. I touched his shoulder, which startled him. "Hey." I sat down beside him.

"Man, these niggas killed my babies. They killed my motherfucking babies. They should've killed me." He broke down crying.

I could hear the grief in his cries and, as bad as I tried, I couldn't help but feel sorry for him. I wanted to find out what happened, but he was in no shape to talk. I rubbed his back and then got up. I walked over to the detectives and Devon. "Do you all know what happened here? I tried talking to Mr. Sanders, but he's too distraught right now."

"From what we gathered from Sanders and the neighbors, a dark Suburban pulled up, and two masked gunmen jumped out and started shooting up the house. One entered the house while the other one went around the back. Your client was the only one not killed. So that is kind of fishy to me." The uniformed officer chuckled.

"Where is your heart at? This man just witnessed his family being gunned down, and you're sitting here, laughing. I'm taking my client away from here, but here is my card. If you all have any questions for him, please don't hesitate to call." I handed the cop one of my cards.

"Damn, somebody has their panties in a bunch."

"Officer Spencer, that's enough," Devon said.

"Well, thank you, because I was just about to dig into his faggot ass," I said and walked off. I hated when a punk tried to show off for his peers.

I breathed hard and walked over to where Javon was holding his head. "Listen, do you have anyone you want me to call for you? You need to get out of here." I was trying to get him away from the scene before the coroner showed up.

"Nah, I can't leave my babies. Plus, I ain't got nowhere to go. This is my life," he managed to say between sobs.

I grabbed his arm. "Listen to me; you need to get out of here. You can't help them; they're gone. You have to worry about yourself, and you know the police are already looking at you."

"Looking at me for what? They think I had something to do with this? What kind of evil nigga do they think I am?" he said while snot rolled down his nose.

"Calm your voice down! Let's go. I already told them to contact me if they needed to talk to you." I walked off with him following closely behind me. "I'm parked over here."

"Malaya! Malaya!" I heard Devon hollering my name.

"Yes, what's up?" I stopped and turned around to face him.

"Be careful with that guy! I know you're only trying to help, but he's a cold-blooded killer, and I'm not sure that he's not the one who set this up."

"Thanks for being concerned, but I'm a big girl, and I can protect myself."

"What the fuck was he saying to you? Why do you seem so mushy wit' that nigga? Ain't that the same nigga who's trying to send a nigga away?" Javon said in an angry tone.

"I've worked alongside District Attorney Williams for years and, yes, he is the prosecutor on your case." I wasn't going to sit here getting interrogated by this nigga. This was probably a mistake. Maybe I should've just left his ass here.

I got in the car and backed out. His eyes were bloodshot, and he just kept staring out into space. His body was in the car, but his mind was definitely far away.

"Where do you want me to drop you?"

"Take me to the south side. I need to see my old head."

"Your old head? Is that your father?"

"Nah. Don't worry 'bout all that."

He had a smart mouth for somebody who needed help. I cut the music up because I was one second away from telling this nigga to get out of my car.

"Let me ask you something. How much money do you need to get the hell out of my life?"

"Man, fuck you, B. You think I want money? I want you to get me off these fucking charges. That's what the fuck I want," he yelled.

"Well, I don't control the courts, so I can only do my best."

"Hmm. Well, you better make sure your best gets me off."

"You know, the more you open your mouth, the more I realize what a bitch-ass nigga you are." After that, I cut the music all the way up! I was fucking done with him and his fucking case!

CHAPTER ELEVEN

Javon

Many days I went without food when I was growing up. Shit, I ain't had anyone to love me as a child because Mama was a whore and Daddy, well, I never met the buster. With that said, I was no stranger to pain. But it ripped my soul out seeing my own flesh and blood lying there lifeless and there wasn't shit I could do to bring them back! My daughter and my son were gone. These niggas could've killed me instead. Shit, I would've lain down, happily, if it would've spared my babies' lives. I took my phone out and scrolled through their pictures. Tears welled up as a sharp pain ripped through my chest. I fell to the ground, holding my chest.

"Noooooooooooooooo! Noooooooooooooooo! God, please take me. Please, God," I pleaded. There was no way I could go on without my babies. I thought I was dying; that's how much I was hurting. I was ready to join my babies.

***

The constant ringing of my cell phone had me feeling tight. I didn't want to rap with anyone. I got up off of the carpeted floor. I looked around. I was in a familiar place, just wasn't too sure where I was. To be honest, I didn't remember how I even got here. My dead kids' faces were so clear in my head. The blood, my li'l man's eyes popped open, all of it. For the first time since their death, I also remembered their mother. I didn't care how much we fought; she was my ride or die. I failed to protect her and my kids. Their blood was on my hands. Oh, my God!

"You woke?" A voice startled me.

I jumped up. I was face to face with my old head, Abraham. "Yeah, I was just—"

"No explanation needed, young blood. Here. Have some of this." He handed me a big rolled blunt.

I snatched it out of his hand and followed him out of the room. "I 'ppreciate it, but I need something stronger than this. I know you got sump'n."

"Sit down."

He grabbed a bottle of Jamaican overproof white rum and poured a glass. I'd never had it before, but I'd heard from a few Jamaican friends that this shit was nothing but the truth. I grabbed the glass and took a big gulp. I started coughing uncontrollably as the liquor stung my throat. I spit that shit out! "Man, what the fuck? You tryin'a kill me?"

"You said you wanted something strong, so I gave you something strong."

"Man, that shit is nasty."

"You're still a baby, young blood." He chuckled.

I could see he was enjoying himself at my expense. He had no idea how I was feeling right now. Joking around was the last thing on my mind.

"Loosen up. I know you're hurting for your offspring."

"Yo, these niggas killed my babies, Abraham."

"Did you see their faces?"

"Nah, but I do know they were the same niggas who tried to kill me."

"How can you be sure?"

"The same vehicle. I'm sure of that. I was this close to the nigga, and I didn't kill him."

"I think somebody has a personal beef with you."

I took a pull of the high-grade weed and passed the blunt to him. "That's what's killing me, though. If a nigga got beef wit' me, they need to come see me. Instead, they're playing pussy and shit. I can't beef wit' a nigga if I don't know who I'm beefing wit'."

He sat there, quiet, smoking and looking in space. "I told you before that your closest enemy could be your best friend, and your best friend can become your worst enemy."

I sat there, pondering the knowledge he was spitting. I wasn't in the mood for no proverbs, but I knew there was a lesson in everything he spoke. He rolled another blunt, and we smoked some more.

"What are your plans? How are you gonna move on from this?"

"I can't even think straight. First, I'ma bury my little soldiers, and then I'm going to declare war on the whole motherfucking city. Somebody knows who these niggas are, and they're gonna talk real soon."

"Don't be foolish! An angry man makes unwise decisions. Calm your nerves, sort out the situation, and then go in for the kill."

"No disrespect, ol' G, but I don't even give a fuck for real. I lost everything that mattered to me in this world. I'm a dead man walking."

"You lost almost e'erything!"

"What do you mean? My bitch and my kids are gone. I ain't got no other family." My eyes started to gather water.

"But you still have your old man."

"What you mean? My old man?" I stood up.

He looked at me and then smiled. He tried to pass me the blunt.

"Nah, fuck that. Answer me. What the fuck you mean by that?" I slapped his hand away.

"Young blood, I'm your daddy—"

Before he could finish his sentence, I punched him in the jaw, knocking the blunt out of his mouth.

"Don't you ever put your motherfucking dick beaters on me again." He pointed his Glock in my face.

"Ha-ha, you got it." I laughed 'cause the old nigga caught me slipping.

He touched his face and rubbed his jawbone. "Now, back to what the fuck I was saying. You're my one and only son. I know this might come as a shocker, but I am your father."

The tears started flowing; I was feeling overwhelmed. I spent my life wishing for a daddy. I used to see my homeboys and them hanging out with their fathers, and I used to wish it was me. Now, here I was, and this old nigga was telling me that he was my daddy. After all these fucking years.

"Son, so many times I wanted to tell you, but I couldn't bring myself to tell you. I was way older than yo' mama, and it was a one-night thing. Years later, I saw her, and she told me I had a son. By then, I was too deep into these streets, and having a son meant that niggas would try to touch him whenever they couldn't get to me. I watched you grow up, and at times, I would drop by and give your grandma a few dollars. I made sure your grandma had money to take care of you. I was always in the shadows, even when you didn't see me."

"The fuck you think I wanted money for, huh? I wanted your love and your time. I needed a dad to teach me how to be a man," I yelled.

"You have the right to be angry with me. I can take it. Go ahead."

I didn't say a word; I just sat there. The tears were drying up because the weed had taken over. I was no longer feeling emotional. Anger was starting to set in. My head felt like it was about to explode.

"Listen, young'un, I ain't been no daddy to you, and I can't change that, but I want you to give me a chance. Right now, all we've got is each other." He squeezed my shoulders.

I didn't say anything; I just sat there. He walked off into his living room.

"Young'un, come in here. I've got something to show you."

I got up and dragged myself into the living room. I flopped down on his leather couch. I had been to his house many times, but this was the first time I was allowed to step foot into the living room.

He threw a stack of paper on my lap. I quickly picked it up and started looking. "Is this some kind of joke?"

"Joke? Nah. Your homeboy is a rat."

"Man, watch how you're talking 'bout my motherfucking brother. He ain't no rat," I snapped.

"Look at the picture! That's him on numerous occasions, working with the fucking feds."

"The feds? What the fuck they want?" I was confused as hell now. My case was state, not federal.

"They want you, the head nigga in charge. Your boy's been working for them for almost a year now."

"Hell nah, not my nigga. You're just tryin'a throw salt on my nigga's name. Hold on. I'm about to hit him up." I grabbed my phone, and that's when it hit me. I had no idea where that nigga was. My mind started racing back to the weeks before I got shot. I stopped by his home, and they had moved. Hell nah, this couldn't be. There was no way my partner, my brother, would work with the feds. This had to be a mistake. But I was sitting here, looking at this nigga getting in a car with a dude who looked like the law. There were pictures of him meeting with them on numerous occasions.

"Who took these pictures, and how did you know this, if it's true?"

"Like I told you, I'm always one step behind you. One day, I followed you, and right after y'all left the trap, I took a second to pull off. Right then, I spotted a car pull up at the trap, and he got in. After that day, I got my right-hand man to start following him. That's how he took all those pics. I then took them to my man on the inside of the feds' investigation, and he confirmed that he is their informant. He is in the witness protection program."

My stomach started growling, and water gathered in my mouth. I got up, threw the pictures on the ground, and ran to the bathroom. I buried my head into the toilet and started to vomit. "Oh, my God!" I killed my little nigga and his mama, all because I thought he was the snitch. My head started spinning. Nigga, you're acting like a bitch, a little voice echoed in my head. I got up, washed my mouth, and walked out of the bathroom. I really didn't feel like talking anymore.

"Ay, if you 'ont mind, I'ma lie down real quick. I'll get up wit' you later."

"Sure."

I walked back into the room I spent the night in. I got on the bed and lay on my back. Everything in my head was one big ball of confusion. How could I be so fucking stupid not to know that Mann-Mann was working with the law? My mind raced back to the last night we hung out. He seemed different, but I thought it was because he was under stress. One thing that popped in my head was him drilling me about what happened. What a bitch. This nigga could've been wearing a wire and, if this was true, I confessed everything to him. I sat up fast and rubbed my hands over my face.

I searched my phone for Plies's song "I Kept It Too Real." That was the only thing I wanted to hear. Tears filled my eyes. I felt betrayed, not because this nigga was working with the people, but because he was working against me, his little brother and his partner. I would've given my life up for this nigga but, in the end, he didn't show me the same love. That nigga better stay hidden 'cause, on my dead kids, if he ever shows his face 'round here anymore, I'ma show him the same love he showed me: none!

Malaya

The police were so predictable. I was on my way to work when my phone rang. It was an officer on the line. He wanted me to bring my client in for questioning. I busted a U-turn and dialed the office number.

"Hello, good morning. Shawrtz and Ipswich Law Firm. How may I help you?"

"Good morning, Dana, it's me."

"Oh, hey, boss lady," she said gleefully.

"Hi. Please reschedule my appointments for later this afternoon. Say around three p.m. if possible."

"All righty, talk to you later."

I hung up and then dialed Javon's number. "Yo," he answered.

"You need to get dressed and meet me down by the station. They want to question you some more about what happened yesterday."

"All right, I'll be there."

I didn't ask him how he was going to get there and, honestly, I didn't really want to know. Last night, I was sure that I was done with his case, but reality kicked in. I needed to get him off so he could get the fuck out of my life for good.

I pulled into the parking lot and waited for about twenty minutes. I saw when a dark 2015 Lexus pulled into the space beside me. I saw when he exited the vehicle. He was looking a hot mess; he had on the same clothes he had on yesterday. I cut my car off, grabbed my briefcase, and got out.

"Have you gotten any kind of rest?"

"Nah, but I'm good, yo. Let's get this over wit'."

"Okay, then. Please remember if they ask you something that you don't remember or if you're not comfortable in answering, let me answer it."

"Shit, I ain't got nothin' to hide," he lied.

Yeah, right.

"Good morning, my name is Attorney Ipswich, and I'm here to see Officer Spencer."

"Good morning. Hold on a sec."

Within a few minutes of waiting, the same rude-ass officer from yesterday came to escort us into one of their interview rooms.

"Man, they asses need to come on already," Javon said.

I was going to respond to him, but I didn't see the need. He was working my last nerves, and I was trying not to be inconsiderate. I had no idea what he was going through. Regardless of how fucked up he was as a person, he was a damn good daddy from what he told me. To witness what he did yesterday could break a strong person down.

Finally, the officers came in the room and started their questioning. I could see on Javon's face that he wasn't feeling it.

"Did you and your woman have any kind of dispute?"

"What the fuck is that supposed to mean? Huh, nigga? You think I killed my fucking kids and their mama?" He got up and flipped the table over, spilling cups of coffee.

"You better sit yo' ass down before I arrest you for disorderly conduct."

"Nah, nigga, fuck you."

"You better sit your ass down and close your mouth," I said as I towered over him.

He looked at me and hissed through his teeth. "Officers, unless you're going to charge my client with something, we're leaving."

As soon as I said that, he got up and walked out the door.

I stayed behind so I could address the officer. I turned to the officer. "You're a real asshole." I didn't wait for a response. I just walked out, slamming the door behind me. I was so pissed off that I almost bumped into Devon.

"Are you all right?"

"Yes, I'm good. You need to really get that asshole, Officer Spencer, under control."

"I'll talk to him."

I walked off on his ass also. I didn't trust any of these motherfuckers in uniform or with a badge.

I noticed Javon standing by his car when I walked outside. "What was that all about inside there?"

"Man, quit playing. You heard how that nigga was talking down at me. That wasn't no damn questioning; that nigga was trying to say I killed my motherfucking kids."

"I was right there with you! There was no need for what you did. You're acting like a madman."

"Well, you know what, bitch? Since you're so cozy with these motherfuckers, fuck you too."

"I'm so over you behaving like a little child. Grow the fuck up, and start taking responsibility for your actions."

"Responsibility, huh, bitch? How about you walk your grown ass in there and take full responsibility for getting your husband killed? That's right, because you're a scary bitch. I see I ain't the only one with dirty hands."

"You know what? I'm done with you! I quit. Please find a different lawyer for your case. I will go the judge and let him know that I can't defend you anymore."

"Suck my dick, bitch! You can't motherfucking quit. It's in your best interest to make sure I beat my case and, I promise you, if I don't, you will regret it."

He winked at me.

I didn't know what this fool was trying to prove, but I wanted no part of it. I looked at him, shook my head, and quickly opened my car door. I got inside, started the car, and pulled off. I couldn't think straight. How did I allow myself to get caught up with this young bum? I knew better than this, but I was so determined to get rid of Trent that I didn't think it through correctly.

I waited for the kids to go to bed. I poured a glass of wine and sat out in my sunroom. This was the place I often came when I needed to clear my head. I wondered how I got here. I was a good person before I met Trent. All I ever wanted was

a man to love me unconditionally; but, after years
of abuse, my heart turned stone cold. And after I
caught him screwing that faggot, I knew I wanted
him dead. There was no way I could live with him,
knowing he was a faggot. I wished he would've
left, but he was determined to make my life hell. I
thought about poisoning him but decided against
it because they would be suspicious, but hell, I
was still being accused even though I didn't pull
the trigger. I thought my plan was a good one, but
somehow, someway, I thought I was their prime
suspect. It didn't help what this fuck nigga was
throwing out there. I wondered if he told anyone
else about what he did.

The thought of poisoning him crossed my
mind also, but that would be suspicious. I took
another sip of my drink as I figured out a way to
get myself out of this shit.

Javon

I should've been taking my kids to the park
or to their favorite spot, Chuck E. Cheese's,
but instead, I was planning their funerals.
Tania's mother and brothers came down from
Albany, New York. This was my second time
seeing her mom, and it wasn't a pleasant visit.
I met her at the funeral home, and that bitch
start yelling that I got her baby killed. I tried
to calm her down, but the closer I got to her,

the more she screamed, "Murderer." People in the funeral home stood there, looking at us.

I tried to explain to this bitch that I loved her daughter and would never do anything to intentionally hurt her. But instead, the bitch hawked some cold spit in my face. I raised my hand to slap that bitch down, but I stopped before it got that far. I wasn't tryin'a get locked up because my bond would've been revoked. Instead, I just talked to the director of the funeral home and left.

Life ain't fair. I couldn't believe my kids were gone, my bitch was gone, and my brother/partner betrayed me. I sped down the street, trying to figure out my next move. A nigga was broke; the police searched the house after the murder and found the safe. After the big bust, that was all the paper I had. Over a hundred grand gone down the fucking drain. I knew I was good to get some work, but my connect wasn't fucking with me after that big bust. I couldn't say I blamed him because he wasn't trying to bring any heat to his camp. Shit, that might be too late. If Mann-Mann was working with the people, I knew he done told them about who we copped our work from.

All I had left were the drawers on my ass; and, shit, I needed to bathe. A nigga nuts were sweaty and shit. "Ha-ha." I had to laugh because this was what a nigga had become.

I didn't want to go back to Abraham's house, but I had nowhere else to go. I hated him for what he did to me, but I knew that right about now I had no one but him. I needed money to bury my kids and to get back on my feet. I wasn't asking the nigga for no handout. I just needed him to throw me some work so I could flip it really quick.

I banged on his back door and waited. I felt naked out here in these streets without my pistol. I was pretty sure that whoever shot me and killed my family was still around.

"Young blood, you can't be banging like you're the police," Abraham said as he opened the door and walked away.

"Oh, my bad."

"How did your interview go?"

"Man, fuck them police. Motherfuckers acting like I was behind that bullshit." I shook my head in disbelief.

"What did you think was gonna happen? These motherfuckers don't give a fuck 'bout you. So, what did your lawyer say?"

"Man, fuck that ho. She sat there and didn't say shit to defend me. I told that bitch fuck her."

"You know you're a grown man, and I can't tell you what to do, but the biggest mistake you made was sleeping with that woman."

"What? Damn, how did you know about her and me?" I was starting to suspect his ass. How the fuck did he know e'erything about my life?

"I told you, I know a little of everything that goes on in this town. I told you to contact that woman to defend you because she's known to have the DA's office in her pocket. A lot of dudes beat their cases or had it dropped to a few years because of her. You done got mixed up with that lady. Did you know they're investigating her for her husband's murder?"

"Huh? What? I ain't know shit."

"That's good, because he was a detective, and you know they ain't goin' to ease up until they pin that murder on somebody."

I was starting to believe that this bitch was bad news from the beginning. I couldn't believe I allowed my dick to get me involved in some cop's murder. That's capital murder.

"You a'ight?"

"Yeah, I'm good! Just thinking it all seems like a dream, these last few days. Like I'm waiting for someone to tap me on my shoulder and say, 'Nigga, wake up.'"

"Well, son, I hate to tell you, this ain't no dream. You're awake, and shit might get worse before it gets better. First things first, I know you're broke, so I've got the kids' funeral. You can take the car you're driving. And if it were any other time, I would've blessed you with some work but, young blood, I can't do that. You're too hot right now, and I can't afford to get caught up in no federal investigation. You know they've been trying to get me for years, so this would be too easy for them."

"What you think, I would tell on you? And I ain't yo' motherfucking son."

"Nah, it ain't that! You just attract the wrong kind of people. You need to chill out, deal with this case, and then move on after that."

Man, fuck that. I wasn't tryin'a hear what he was saying. I was a grown man; I couldn't go on living off of no other nigga. This nigga goin' to make me fuck around and rob his ass. I quickly dismissed that thought. This nigga had always had my back; plus, he was nothing nice to be fucked with.

We ended up drinking and smoking blunts after blunts. This nigga was kind of a cool dude. I just wished I knew that he was my dad when I was growing up.

"Well, young blood, I'm about to call it a night."

"A'ight, yo!"

After he left for bed, I got up and walked to the refrigerator and grabbed another beer. I sat back down on the floor, just letting my thoughts run wild. I thought a heard a sound, so I got up and walked to the window. I looked outside and didn't see anything. I fixed the curtain and walked away. I was thinking how late it was; but, before I could finish my thought, I heard glass shattering followed with gunshots everywhere. I dove over the sofa. I heard footsteps coming down the back and shots fired from a mini 14 assault rifle. I knew it was Abraham because he often bragged about his chopper. It was like Desert Storm up in the house, and then the shooting stopped. I wanted to pop my head up, but I wasn't sure who was alive and who wasn't.

"Youngblood, you in here?"

"Yeah, I'm here." I popped my head up and saw Abraham standing over a nigga's body. "Here, let me hold this. Let me check if anybody else is in here." I took the Glock from him and walked to the front of the house. I didn't see anyone else. I hurried back to the living room. I was curious to see who the fuck this nigga was. Hopefully, I could get the answers that I needed. I aimed the gun at his head, just in case he wasn't dead. I removed the ski mask from his face. I took a step back! This was the nigga D. Drizzle's big brother, who was supposed to be doing a bid in the penitentiary. "Fuck," I said out loud.

I was knocked off my square for a quick second and, before I could regroup, I heard a voice. "Nigga, drop the gun and put your hands up."

I felt a gun pressed against my head. I tried to weigh my options. Did I want to drop my gun, or did I want to risk it and just turn around and shoot this nigga?

"Pussy hole bwoy, I say drop the bumboclaat gun," he said in a raw Jamaican accent.

"Not before you do, my nigga!" I heard Abraham's voice echo.

"Go suck you bomboclaat muma," he said to no one in particular.

I heard two thumps, and then he fell to the ground. Abraham shot him in the head twice. He lay on the ground with half of his face gone. Blood was splattered everywhere from the high-power rifle.

"Yo, give me that gun and get out of here."

"What? These niggas ran up in here."

"I know that, but I need to call in my cleaning crew, and I don't need you around any of this. Now, you need to go on. Go get you a room and lie low. I've got to get this place cleaned up."

"A'ight," I said reluctantly.

He handed me a stack of bills, and I grabbed the keys and ran out the back door. None of this made sense. Why would the nigga want me dead? We were not really cool, but the nigga showed respect. I dragged my memory back to the day when I killed his little brother and mother. I thought they were the only ones in the apartment, but now it had me wondering if he was there. I checked the house, so how did I miss him? And now, he retaliated and killed my family.

"Oh, God, no." I hit the steering wheel, which jerked the car. Why did I not think about this before? Tears fell from my eyes as I had to admit that my kids were dead because of some shit that I did. What's crazy is that my little nigga got killed for nothing. He wasn't even the fucking rat. I remember how pleading his eyes were when he begged for his life.

A car horn honked! I looked up and realized I was out of my lane and almost hit another car. I pulled over to the side of the street. It was dangerous for me to keep driving. I needed a second to regroup! I pulled up my kids' pictures in my phone. I rubbed my hand over the screen of my phone. "Daddy is so sorry; I swear I'm sorry." I hugged my phone as if it were my babies.

"God, I need them back. Please, God. I will trade my life, God. Here take me," I yelled out.

I started questioning if there was a God. I had no understanding why He would keep me here and let my babies die. They never hurt anyone; they were innocent.

I finally mustered up some energy to pull off. I needed to find a room. I decided to stop at the liquor store and buy a bottle of Cîroc Coconut, and then I grabbed a few blunts. I was about to get fucked up. It would've been nice if I had a bitch to join me but, nah, I was good on that right now.

I must've slept three days straight. I noticed I missed several calls from that bitch, Malaya! I had no idea what that ho wanted. The last time I saw her, she told me to get a new lawyer. Now, she was blowing a nigga up. I bet her ass was missing a nigga and wanted to get her back beat out. Any other time, I would be willing to tear that pussy up, but not this time. I was done with that bitch, professionally and personally.

It's funny how things become clear when I was high as hell. My entire life was built on loyalty and riding for niggas. I done killed for my niggas and broke bread with these same niggas. But, in the end, not one of these niggas rode for me or held me down. Here I was, sitting in a cold world, all by myself. Who the fuck could I run to now that I was down and out? No-fucking-body at all! I was done feeling sorry for myself. There wasn't much left for me here. Friday was the day that my kids would be laid to rest, and then after that, it was whatever. I wasn't even worried about beating my case anymore. This might sound fucked up, but for once Javon was going do something that benefited just him.

I woke up bright and early. I had a plan that had to be executed the right way. I searched through e'erything to find that detective's card, but I couldn't find it. I must've left it at Abraham's crib. I got dressed and decided to go to his house. I hadn't seen him since the day of the incident.

He opened the door, and I walked in. "I thought I told you to lie down and not come around."

"I know, but I left a paper in the room; plus, I needed to check on you, make sure you good."

"Ha-ha, I'm good. One thing I know to do is defend what's mine. These young niggas don't want no beef with this old fool." He chuckled.

"I see," I said and walked toward the room.

I closed the door and started going through my bag that I had my clothes in. I didn't see the card. I was starting to get frustrated. I threw all the clothes back in the bag, grabbed my two pairs of sneakers, and was about to walk out the room when I noticed the card on the ground. I picked it up, put it in my pocket, and walked out.

"Ay, I need to holla at you."

I dropped the bag and stood there. "What's good?"

"I 'ont want you to take this the wrong way, but I'ma need you to get your own place. I'm too old for drama and to spend the rest of my life in prison. That's why I'm solo, 'cause I don't do the streets. I'm going to give you money to get back on your feet, and I want you to know I love you. Even though we ain't got no father-and-son relationship, I love you, and I got your back, but it's best if we just stay apart while you have open cases and shit."

"Damn, I was just about to tell you that I'm about to bounce, but I see how it is, Dad. You couldn't wait to kick a nigga out."

"Get out your feelings, young'un. You're a street nigga, so you should feel where I'm coming from. I can't take no heat 'round here. Here goes ten stacks. Take it and start over." He handed me some money.

"You think that what I want is money? Nigga, I had money, and trust and believe when this shit is over, I'ma bounce back. You're throwing money at me like I'm a bitch. Nah, old head, you keep that. I'm good, my G."

I walked off before any more words were spoken. This was a nigga I'd loved since I was a little boy. Ain't nothing changed, but I was hurt that he would try to pay me to stay out of his life. It wasn't new, though; even the bitch who birthed me didn't stick around.

I threw the bag into the trunk. I knew this was my last time seeing him. I took one last look at the house before pulling off.

This wasn't what I wanted to do, but a nigga was drowning, and there was no way out. It was either this bitch or me and, the way I saw it, the bitch had to wear it. I dialed the detective's number that was on the card.

"Hello," he answered, breathing all heavy in the phone.

I thought about hanging up, but I quickly decided to go ahead with my plan. "This is Javon. I don't know if you remember me."

"Oh, yes. Javon Sanders, right? What can I do for you, Mr. Sanders?"

"Well, when I saw you at the hospital, you said you would be interested in making a deal with me."

"Yes, yes, yes. Will your lawyer be with you?"

"Nah, I need to do this by myself."

"Okay, sure. Well, can you meet today?"

"Yeah, I'm on my way to my hotel room. You can meet me there."

"Okay, great. My partner will accompany me if you don't mind."

"Yeah, he's cool."

I gave him the address and hung up. Make no misunderstanding, I didn't trust these niggas. I thought long and hard about this move that I was making, and as fucked up as it may have seemed to everybody else, it was needed. My children were gone, and I needed to get far away from here. Being locked up would only stunt my growth and tear a nigga down.

I was going to smoke, but I decided to do it after these niggas left. I sat waiting on them to show up. I got everything straight in my head. At the end of the day, I wasn't the one who pulled the trigger!

CHAPTER TWELVE

Malaya

I spoke to my mother this morning. No matter how I was feeling, she always found the right words to soothe my soul. I could never get enough of my mother's love. I loved New York, but I was happy to make this move to Maryland. I was tired of being up here by myself, plus my girls would love it out there in Maryland. Mama gave me the number for the real estate agent she used. I was going to miss Dana and Isiah, but it was time for a change.

It was hard getting the other house sold because of Trent's murder. A lot of people remembered it because it was all over the news. Hopefully, a family would look past that, and buy it. It was a beautiful home; all it needed was a great family.

I was off today, so I decided to do some cleaning. I heard my phone ringing, and I ran upstairs to grab it. It was Isiah, so I answered. "Hey, babe," I said jokingly.

"Hey, Malaya." He wasn't his usual flamboyant self.

"What's the matter, Isiah?"

"I just spoke to the DA. They want me to take you in for questioning."

"What the hell do you mean? About what?"

"They want to question you about Trent's death. They supposedly have a break in the case."

"That's ludicrous. If they had a break, why do they need me to come in? I swear to God I'm going to sue the entire department for harassment. When do they want us in there?"

"By three p.m."

"All righty."

I hung the phone up and threw it on the ground. I was fucking sick of these motherfuckers. What the fuck did they want from me? I done told their asses over and over, I ain't had shit to do with my husband's death. Why couldn't they just fucking believe me? My nerves were shot. I thought of not going in, but I knew that would just have damn near every cop in this city looking for me. My kids were at school, so I couldn't go anywhere even if I wanted to.

I picked out a pair of jeans and a nice collared shirt. I then took a quick shower. I didn't like the way I was feeling, but I was a boss bitch. I could handle any- and everything that came my way. I applied some lip gloss and grabbed my purse.

I parked in the rear and walked to the front. I spotted Isiah sitting in the front. I walked over to him.

"Hey, love," he greeted me and gave me a tight hug.

"Thank you so much. I needed that."

"I'm your lawyer, but I'm more your friend. Let's go in here." He held my hand, and we walked in.

"Yes, Attorney Shawrtz and Attorney Ipswich. We have a meeting with the DA."

"Sure. Follow me to our interview room."

We walked in and sat down. Funny, this was the same room Javon and I were in days ago. Speaking of Javon, I hadn't heard from him since the day of the interview. I tried calling him but got no response.

"Hello," Devon said as he walked in with the two detectives who kept harassing me. "Mrs. Ipswich, I asked your attorney to bring you in as a courtesy. As a colleague, I think it's best this way. All right, this is what we have. We have an indictment for you."

"An indictment?"

"Hold on, Mrs. Ipswich, let me handle this."

"Yes. We took the evidence to a grand jury, and she was indicted today."

He handed a copy of the indictment to Isiah. "Indicted on one count of criminal solicitation of capital murder. Two counts of hindering apprehension."

My head started to spin, and my chest tightened. Was I hearing this right? They were charging me with criminal solicitation? Shouldn't they have been charging me with murder instead? I was confused; too much was happening too fast.

"Who did I solicit to get killed? I thought I was here to get questioned about Trent's death."

"You are. Hello, wife!"

I was frozen! How? How? I couldn't get any words out. My tongue felt heavy as I tried to find the words that I wanted to use. I stood up, but my knees buckled underneath me. The walls around me started closing in. I knew then I was dying. I needed to die because someone was playing a horrible joke on me. One that I didn't think was funny at all.

"Are you okay, Mrs. Ipswich?"

"Huh?" I looked around, and all focus was on me.

"Hello, Malaya," Trent said, confirming any doubts that I had about him being dead.

"How? You're dead. I saw you lying there in blood. I buried you. I watched them put . . ." I couldn't finish my sentence because I didn't actually see them put him in the ground. I left before they got to that point.

"Detective, please explain. If this is a joke, it's not funny at all," Isiah stood up and demanded.

"Well, I can explain," the district attorney I'd been fucking said.

So, this nigga was in on this terrible joke. I shot him a look that could cut his soul out.

"Well, Mr. Ipswich is not dead, as you can see. We got word that Mrs. Ipswich here was looking for someone to kill her husband. So, the detectives and the district attorney's office came up with a plan."

"A fucking plan. I never wanted Trent dead. We had our problems, but we were working on it. Tell them, Trent. Tell them." I got up and tried to walk to my husband.

"Sit down, Mrs. Ipswich. Mr. Ipswich here was shocked when we told him of your plans. He thought we were trying to set you up. So, this was all our doing."

I saw blood on him. I had blood on my clothes. None of this shit made sense.

"My client knew nothing about this, and these are serious allegations. I will be filing court papers first thing in the morning. Y'all have no evidence that my client knew anything about this."

"Trent, say something. Please tell them I couldn't do this to you. This is me, your wife,

Malaya. Tell them," I begged, but he stood there looking at me with a disgusted kind of look plastered across his face.

That's when it really hit me; this nigga didn't give a damn about what I was saying. He was on their side. He knew about this and pretended the entire time.

"Mrs. Ipswich, you're under arrest for the soliciting the murder of Trent Ipswich and hindering apprehension. You have the right to—"

"I know my fucking rights. I just hope you all know y'all rights! Because I will be coming for each one of you and your bosses."

"Take her out of here."

"Isiah, get me out of here immediately."

"I'm on it."

A detective led me out of the office. There was a crowd of officers standing there, whispering and shaking their heads. I hung my head down as he led me away.

I was led off like a common criminal, me, a woman with great pride. How could they do this to me? I was sure that they didn't have anything on me because I never talked to anyone about this outside of Javon. There was no way he went to them and told them what happened; or did he?

I was searched and fingerprinted. I was tearing up inside, but I held my composure. I'd learned never to let people see me sweat. These were serious charges, which most times no bond was granted for, but I wasn't a criminal, so I was sure I would be bonded out.

I was able to go in front of the judge over live video. I could see the strange look on the judge's face when he read my name and saw my face. I wasn't in the mood to entertain him, so I sat there quietly, listening to him as he read my charges. He gave me bond in the amount of $300,000.

"I'm about to get on it asap," Isiah said.

"All right."

"Babe, hold your head up. You will be out of that hell hole real soon."

I appreciated his support because he was the only one in my corner right now.

I was placed in a dingy, pissy-smelling cell along with two bitches who looked like they were coming down off crack binges. I wasn't going to sit down, not for one second, on that bench. All kinds of thoughts were running through my head, but I tried to remain positive.

The guard came around passing out sandwiches, which I didn't want. "Miss, can you get the sandwich and give it to me 'cause I'm hungryyyyy," this dirty-looking bitch with little to no teeth touched my shoulder and said.

"Don't touch me!" I said angrily.

"Damn, bitch, all I was trying to do was get the sandwich."

"Well, this bitch doesn't give a damn if you eat or not." I moved away from her. There wasn't that much space, but it gave that bitch and me a great little distance. See, bitches see me all dressed up, so they let these looks fool them.

I was getting antsy. I wondered what was taking so long. I needed to be bonded out before the bus came to take the prisoners to the county jail. I had no intentions of bringing my black ass there.

"Malaya Ipswich," I heard a guard holler before she walked to the cell and opened it. I could've run over that bitch with the way I rushed out of the cell. It was about time they got me the hell up out of there.

Javon

After making my statement to the detectives, I was asked to come to the station to be briefed by the district attorney. It was one thing to talk to these niggas in the hotel room, but it was a whole different ballgame when I was asked to walk up in a police station. These niggas didn't give a fuck about my life as long as they got what they wanted.

I thought about saying nah, but I was already in too deep, and I was afraid that if I backed out, my charges wouldn't be dropped. The decision wasn't hard to make since the bitch left me for dead. She knew I had a case and still chose to walk away from me.

I searched for a parking space, all the way in the back of the station. I couldn't risk being seen by any niggas who knew me. I planned on hitting the streets when this shit was over, so keeping my name clean was everything. I walked in and gave the secretary my name. I took a seat, but I wasn't feeling comfortable. Every time I came close to a police station I got nervous.

"Mr. Sanders, come on with me. I'm happy you could make it."

I nodded my head to show recognition. I didn't trust this nigga and his friendly ways. I knew this was how they operated when they wanted information out of a person. I played along with them, but I kept them at a good distance. We walked into a room where the DA and another nigga was. I'd never met him nor did I know who he was.

"Gentlemen, this is Javon Sanders. I invited him down here so we can get a formal statement plus explain to him where we will be going from here."

"Hello, Javon. My name is Trent Ipswich!" the stranger said and got up and tried to shake my hand.

"Who are you?" For some reason, I felt like something wasn't right. I searched my brain real fast. I wondered where I had seen this nigga before.

"This is the man you were supposed to kill."

"Supposed to kill? What the fuck are you talking about?" See, this fuck nigga was playing games and shit. These niggas were only playing with me because they knew I didn't have my pistol.

"You heard correct. See, you weren't totally honest with us about what happened. What you failed to mention was that you were not the one who shot Detective Ipswich. Your good friend was the one who walked into the house that night. I know you are trying to figure out what the hell is going on, so let me run it by you. We knew that Malaya wanted you to kill her husband, and you, in turn, told your boy. We found out about this, so we staged the murder scene. As you can see, he is alive and kicking."

"You all played me! Y'all knew this nigga wasn't dead, but y'all came at me like y'all were investigating a fucking murder! Y'all fucked me raw like a bitch!"

I scooted down in my chair; I'd never felt so fucking low before in my life. This was a setup from the gate. The only other person who knew about the plan to kill the nigga was my ex-partner. My mind raced back to the day he begged me to let him handle it. I now saw it wasn't because he was looking out for me; it was because he was trying to save the nigga from getting killed.

"I'm about to bounce up outta here. I can't believe I let y'all pussy niggas play me like this. Everything was a fucking lie. Y'all used me to make a case; y'all ain't have no case." I laughed, not because shit was funny but because I fucked up.

"Sit down, Mr. Sanders. We're not finished here," the DA boy said while he looked through a folder.

"Nah, we're done. I came in here voluntarily. Remember?"

"I said sit down, unless you want me to slap this charge on you."

"What fucking charge? Shit, the nigga ain't dead and, you said it yourself, I wasn't the one who did the fake killing." I stood up. I was done for real. I turned to walk out.

I heard a voice; it was mine. I turned around; there was mini recorder on the table. I took a step closer. It was my and Mann-Mann's voices on there. I quickly realized that it was the night we met up at the club and were talking. The same night that my dumb ass confessed to him that I killed D. Drizzle and his mother. It was like a sharp knife kept sticking me in open wounds over and over again. Sweat started forming on my forehead as my body temperature rose. I wanted to grab the police gun and start busting at these niggas, but I knew that I wouldn't make it out alive.

The DA cut the tape off and then spoke. "Yes, that's right. That's you on this recording, discussing the brutal murder of one of your codefendants and his mother. I don't have to tell you that if convicted of your previous charges and this murder, you will be gone for the rest of your life. The only way I see out of all this is if you tell us everything about the plan to murder Detective Ipswich and also if you're willing to take the stand and testify against Mrs. Ipswich."

I sat there, staring at this nigga! Was this what my life had become? The same thing I despised I'd become myself: a fucking rat. On the outside, it looked like everything was all right but, inside, that shit was eating me up.

"What is it going to be, Mr. Sanders?" the fuck nigga detective boy said.

I wanted to yell, fuck you, nigga, but I knew better. I knew they were not playing fair, and if I reneged on my word, they would toast my ass. My decision was easy.

"The deal is still on the table? Before I say another word, I need it in writing: that I'm getting full immunity on e'erything."

"All right, let's roll. First, you need to talk; then we will decide if it's a deal that we want," the DA said.

It took me forty minutes to spill my guts about any- and everything they wanted to know. During that time, I blocked out everything I learned in the streets about loyalty and the "no snitching" code. A nigga snitched on me and didn't think twice, so why should I be worried about snitching on a bitch I was only fucking?

Malaya

I signed the bond papers and walked out of the jail. My car was still parked outside because they didn't have a chance to tow it yet. As soon as I walked out, I saw Isiah and Dana. I wished he hadn't brought her in on this, but what the heck? I didn't have much of a choice. She was very sharp and knew the business well, so she might become a very valuable asset on my case.

"Hey, baby." She ran to me and hugged me. I hugged her back, not because I was happy to see her ass but because my ass was happy to be out of jail.

"Hey, diva." Isiah hugged me.

"Hey, hon. Thank you for getting me out so quick. I almost died up in that hell hole," I exclaimed.

"You didn't drop the soap, did you?" Isiah joked and winked at me.

"Ha-ha. I see you've got jokes. I'm just happy I didn't make it down to the jail."

"Malaya, we really need to discuss this case against you."

"I know, but I'm tired, and I need to get home and take care of my children. Matter of fact, I need to let them know their daddy is not dead. It was all a sham so they could get me caught up in some conspiracy bullshit."

"Malaya, listen to me. I need you not to have any contact with Javon Sanders, business or personal," Dana said.

"What are you talking about?" I shot her a strange look.

"This is off the record, but I'm pretty sure Isiah will get this info really soon. He is the one who gave them this information. He told the DA you asked him to kill Trent, and I heard he is cooperating one hundred percent with them."

I thought I was not hearing her correctly. I looked at Isiah and then back at Dana. They both had the same serious look on their faces. "You've got to be kidding me." I looked for a hint of joking on her face, but there was none.

"No. According to my source, while Javon was in the hospital they approached him, and he fell for it, apparently to save his own ass."

"That nigga is a criminal; why would I trust him? He is a liar; I never asked him to kill my husband. I can't believe this shit," I yelled out.

"The DA believes they have a solid case against you."

"I don't give a damn what the DA believes. I know I'm innocent, and I intend to prove it. If I wanted Trent dead, I would've killed him my-damn-self, not ask a nigga who already had a criminal case going on. I'm not no fool; I know the law."

"We're going to beat these charges. In the meantime, I need you to stay away from Mr. Sanders. Don't talk to him or discuss your case with him or anyone else outside of Dana and me. In the meantime, I think you need to stay away from the firm. Let us handle everything."

"I love doing what I do. I have clients who are depending on me," I lashed out.

"I understand that, but those clients will be all right. You need to worry about you. These are some serious charges that can put you behind bars for a very long time. I need you to be focused on Malaya and not on everybody else."

I knew what he was saying made a lot of sense, but I was stubborn.

"Listen, I've got to go. I'll call you in the morning. Thanks, Dana. We'll talk in the a.m. also."

I walked away and walked toward my car. I opened the door and got in. I was physically and mentally drained. I wished I had somewhere to go so I wouldn't have to face the girls. How would I begin to tell them that their daddy wasn't dead, but I was charged with a terrible crime? I felt a terrible migraine coming on. I massaged my temple, trying to ease the pain.

I made it home just in time. As soon as I pulled up, the girls were getting off their bus. I opened the door and walked inside, leaving the door open for them. I heard when they entered the house. I was nervous because I wasn't sure how I was going to start this conversation.

"Hey, Mama," Nyesha yelled.

"Hey," Myesha said.

I walked into the living room. "Girls, I need to talk to both of you."

"I'm tired, plus I've got homework," Myesha said and attempted to walk away.

"I said I need to talk to both of you. Now!"

They both sat on the couch, looking at me. I sat on the couch across from them. "Girls, I have something serious to talk to you all about."

"All right," Myesha said with an attitude.

I decided to say what the fuck I was saying before I ended up choking this grown-ass child sitting in front of me. "Today, I was arrested."

"Arrested for what?" Nyesha blurted out.

"Probably for killing Daddy," Myesha said.

"Stop saying that! Mama didn't kill Daddy. Grandma and them have you brainwashed."

"Shut up! Both of you!" I screamed. "Anyway, I was arrested today. The police are saying I had something to do with your father's botched murder. I say botched because your daddy is not dead. I saw him today. No, he was not shot and killed."

"Daddy is alive? Where is he?" Myesha jumped up off of the couch and stepped toward me.

"You better sit your ass down. Yes, he is alive, and now I've been accused of trying to kill him."

"Mama, they know it's not true, right? I saw Daddy; he was dead."

"Baby, obviously somebody wanted your daddy dead, so the police believe it's me. I'm just telling y'all this before anyone else does. They staged your daddy's murder. I saw him today. He's alive and kicking."

Myesha got up, shot me a dirty look, and walked off. Nyesha got up and ran over to me, hugging me.

"Mama, you have to beat these charges. I know you didn't do this. I swear, Mama, I will always be here with you. We're gonna fight, and we're gonna beat these charges."

My eyes teared up as I listened to my baby girl. How could two girls who were so identical be so different? I hugged her as tight as I could. Even though she wasn't aware, her words just gave me the strength I needed!

The next morning, I had to be in court for my preliminary hearing, and the judge gave me a strict warning to stay away from Trent. I looked at the judge and wondered what the fuck he was on. What in God's name would I be talking to Trent's ass for? That nigga set me up.

After court, I talked with Isiah for a little before I walked off. He might have been the lawyer, but I was going to be the one controlling my defense. I was good at what I did, and I wasn't going to let someone else take control of my destiny.

I was about to get on the elevator when I spotted Devon. "I need to talk to you," I said as he walked by.

He stopped and gave me this nervous look. "You know I can't talk to you." He looked around suspiciously.

"What do you mean? We're friends, right?"

"Malaya, we're friends. I'm sorry. I just can't lose my job behind this."

"Lose your job? You have an issue with talking to me, but you don't have one when you're sticking your dick in me."

"I'm sorry! I have to go." He walked away.

"Fuck you!" I said out of frustration.

I was pissed off that, out of everyone, he would behave like that with me. I was fighting for my freedom, and he was worried about a fucking job. I smiled at the irony of all of this. Let's see how much longer he will have that job.

Javon

I stopped by the funeral home to drop off the rest of the money to the director. I was grateful that I had enough to pay if off. I was forever indebted to Abraham for going out of his way and throwing me that ten stacks. I still had the rest of the money stashed away in my hotel room. I was holding on to it so that when all of this shit was over, I'd have money to bounce back off.

Even though I couldn't stand Tania's mother, I was happy she took over the planning of the funeral. God knows I wasn't in the shape to plan one, so the bitch was good for something besides running her mouth. She also told me of her plan to cremate her daughter so she could put her on her dresser. I did miss her, but I had too much shit to worry about right now. She was dead and didn't have to worry about anything else.

I spent the rest of the evening drinking, smoking, and indulging in self-pity until I passed out. I tried not to break down, but my soul was hurting. I knew I was a piece of shit human being, but I was damn good father.

I was up bright and early. I sat in the corner of my hotel room, just staring at the different pictures of my kids and me. I had over a hundred pictures of them, from the time they were small. I looked at my little man, and it took my memory to the day when he was born. I smiled. I remembered how scared I was. I thought I would break him because he looked so fragile. I smiled because he had brought so much happiness to my life. I felt myself getting teary-eyed, so I got up and put the phone down. I took a shower and got dressed. The funeral services were set to begin in another hour. I wished I didn't have to go, but there was no way I would miss that chance. I was present for their births, and

I would be there when they descended into the ground, because I was their daddy.

I was surprised to see how the hood came out to show support. I thought that after I caught my case, they ain't fuck wit' a nigga no more, but I was wrong. From the chicks I done fucked or was just cool with to the niggas I dealt with before, they were all out, showing their respect to my little soldiers. I also noticed the detectives in the midst. I didn't even look their way for fear that someone might see and jump to the conclusion that I was tight with the police.

I tried my best to be strong; plus, I didn't want to break down in front of people. A few dope boys came up to me and let me know that if I ever needed them, they had me. It gave me hope because I felt like the hood turned their backs on a nigga. I looked around to see if Abraham might've came through, even though I knew that the chances were slim to none. I'd never seen him outside of that house before. I was only hoping he would've made an exception. After all, they were his blood.

I managed not to shed a tear today, even though I was tearing up inside. I knew they were still here with their daddy, no matter what. I grabbed me something to eat and a few bags of powder. I tried powder years ago, but Tania found out and made me promise not to ever do that shit again, and I didn't, until now. I loved smoking weed, but this pain I was feeling called for something stronger. I also bought a bottle of Cîroc and a few blunts. I needed to get my mind off my children and focus on a much a happier time.

I sat at the table in the room and took out a bag of the powder cocaine and emptied it in a one dollar bill. I took my first sniff of the powder. Nothing happened. I then took another sniff, and that's when the magic started. The drug illuminated my brain, and I suddenly felt happy. All that sadness I felt a few minutes ago disappeared that fast. I started laughing at how much I missed the euphoric feeling, the feeling that made me feel like I could conquer the world. I kept sniffing until every drop I had on that money was gone. I was high out of my freaking mind. It was a good high, though; this was what I needed to get through this pain.

I was lying on the bed, enjoying my high, when I heard a banging on the door. It kind of startled me. I jumped up and grabbed the dollar bill and crumbled it up. I looked through the peephole, and I realized it was Abraham. What the fuck is he doing here? I never told him where I was staying.

I thought about ignoring the door and just pretending I wasn't in there, but I was curious to see what he wanted. Like I said earlier, I had never seen him out of that house before. I opened the door and let him in. "Hey, Dad," I said gleefully.

"Young Killa," he said and walked inside the room.

I closed the door behind us. "What a pleasant surprise. How did you know where I was?"

"I told you, I know a lot," he emphasized.

I didn't like how he said that, but I was too high to address anything. I took a seat in the chair, just staring down at the carpet.

"So, what can I do for you, Dad?"

He took a seat by the edge of the bed; I noticed he was dressed in all black, even down to the gloves he was wearing.

"How was the funeral?"

"It was a'ight. You know?"

"You know, son, my whole life I lived in these streets, and I've seen all kinds of shit, but I've always kept my nose clean. I'm from the old school where talking to the police is a crime within itself."

"A'ight, what's all of this?" I wasn't in the mood for no proverbs today. As a matter of fact, I was ready for him to go so I could go back to handling my business.

"I thought you was a G, a real thoroughbred, so you had to know how disappointed I was when I found out you were a fucking rat. My flesh and blood is a snitch!"

"Man, what the fuck are you talking 'bout? I ain't no fucking rat. I live in these motherfucking streets, and I don't fuck wit' no police," I stood up and yelled.

"I told you, I know everything that goes down in this town, and I know you are running your mouth to the detectives about that lawyer bitch. I know you're the reason why she's locked up. Ain't no bitch in my blood, so I know there's no way you can possibly be mine. I came here to kill you, but talking to you changed my mind. I'm gonna let you live so you can suffer in the worst way. After the police use you and throw you away like the piece of garbage you are, I will run you out of this town. No one will ever do business with you again, and if you ever mention my name to them, I promise you, you will be killed, and your body will never be found." He stared me in the eyes.

"Old nigga, you threatening me? Big mistake. I ain't no bitch, and I will dead you if I have to. Believe that! Now, get the fuck out of my room, and just know that this is my motherfucking town. You should see how the hood came out to support a nigga," I bragged.

"Hmmm. They will know really soon that you're a fucking rat. Let's see how much love you get then. I don't make threats, Young Bitch!" He got up, put his Kangol hat on, opened the door, and walked out.

I sat there, furious. How dare this bitch-ass nigga come up in my shit and threaten my life? I needed to get my life back because niggas thought 'cause I was going through some shit, I was a pussy. Fuck that nigga. I might be a rat, but ain't no bitch in my blood. I pulled out my second bag of powder I was determined not to let anyone fuck up my high.

Just when I thought this shit was almost over, the fucking DA's office wanted me to wear a fucking wire while I talked to Malaya. See, these niggas were taking me for a soft bitch. I hadn't spoken to this bitch since the last time I saw her, and now they expected me to call her and get her to admit that she wanted that nigga dead. I tried to tell them that I didn't want to do it, not because I gave a fuck about the bitch, but because I didn't want to face her. The DA quickly reminded me that I didn't have a choice. So, just like an obedient bitch, I agreed.

Malaya

"Hello," I answered.

"Hey, hon. Turn the news on," Dana said.

"What station?"

"Channel 7 Eyewitness News."

I grabbed my remote and turned to the news. Obviously, someone tipped off the news station, and they were covering the story. I saw my picture in the top right-hand corner as she talked about the prominent attorney who was caught up in a love triangle. My heart sank as I watched the horrible things they were saying about me. I knew the entire town, and my peers had heard about this by now.

"I'm so sorry, Malaya."

"Yeah, me too." I hung up the phone.

I scooted down on the carpet in the living room. Everything that I worked so hard for was slipping away from me. How could I survive this shame and embarrassment? I could only imagine the conversation these other lawyers were having about me. "What did I do?" I cried as I laid my head down.

My phone started ringing. I wondered which one of my uppity so-called friends done saw the news and was now calling to be inquisitive. I wasn't in the mood, and whoever it was was going to get cursed the fuck out.

I reached up and over the couch and grabbed my phone. "Hello," I answered without looking at the caller ID.

"Yo, Malaya. What's good?"

I knew I didn't hear what I just heard. This snitch-ass nigga was on my phone. "What the fuck do you want?"

"I just want to talk to you. I heard you got locked up earlier."

"Okay, and what the fuck does that have to do with you?"

"Man, I didn't call for all that! I just called to check up on you and to let you know that they're just trying to set you up. I 'ont know what they told you, but they're just trying to play us against one another. I ain't tell them people shit."

I smiled to myself. I knew this bum knew that I was a lawyer, and I knew how the police rolled. "Javon, I'm a bit lost. What are you talking about, honey?"

"Yo, I 'ont want to say it over the phone, but you know how you asked me to kill your husband?" he said.

"Javon, Javon, honey, listen. I think you've got the wrong person, or I don't know what kind of stunt you're trying to pull. I love my husband. I would never do such a thing. I know I fucked you good and you fell for me, but never in a million years would I think that you would try to kill Trent. I'm sorry if you thought that's what I wanted. I love my husband," I said in my most convincing voice.

"Man, you're tripping. Why are you denying this? You remember—"

I ended the phone call before he got a chance to continue with that foolery. I knew he was wired or the police were somewhere close by. Who the fuck did this amateur nigga think he was playing with? Just because I gave him the pussy and sucked his dick a few times didn't mean I was a dumb bitch.

It also proved to me that the police case against me was weak, and they would go to extremes to try to build a case against me.

I was up bright and early; I finally decided to file for divorce. I was tired of keeping up this charade with Trent. This was my money, and I was taking every fucking dime of it. When I was done, this nigga was going to wish he were dead.

I walked into Baron and Lexington Law Firm. This was a husband-and-wife team, and they were among some the best divorce lawyers in the state. The wife, Shawnda, and I were college roommates, and we kept in touch after law school.

"Good morning. I'm here to see Shawnda Baron," I walked up to receptionist and said.

"Good morning. Do you have an appointment with Mrs. Baron?"

"No, I don't. This is more of a personal visit."

"Okay. Mrs. Baron is on a call right now, but I will let her know that you're here. Please have a seat."

"Thanks."

I took a seat with my legs crossed. It'd been years since I'd seen her, but we were the kind of friends who didn't have to see each other on the regular; but, when we did, we usually picked up right where we left off.

"Malaya," I heard Shawnda's cheery voice yell out.

I got up and saw her walking toward me. "Hey, there, Shawnda. How are you?" I gave her a hug.

"Oh, my, it's been years since we've laid eyes on each other, and I have to tell you, you haven't aged one bit."

"Girl, I have to say the same about you."

"Child, stop it. This is all the work of my plastic surgeon." She laughed. "Follow me. My office is back here."

I followed her into a huge office with a big table. I could see by the look of things that they were definitely making money.

"Sit down. Please."

"Thank you! Shawnda, this is not a social visit."

"Okay, so what can I help you with?"

"Well, I know you saw that I was arrested two days ago. The police are suggesting that I tried to kill Trent, which is completely false."

"Yes, I was shocked when I heard about that."

"Anyway, I'm here because I know you're the best at what you do. I need to divorce him before this case goes to trial. As you know, most of the money belongs to me and, I hate to be blunt, but I don't want his ass to get anything he didn't enter this marriage with."

"I understand. So you know I need to know how the marriage was."

"The first few years were great but, after that, he became abusive, physically and mentally. Then, the cheating started. The last straw was when I walked in and caught him screwing another man in our bed."

"These are some serious allegations; do you have any proof of this?"

I dug into my purse and pulled out my phone. I searched for the video and then handed her the phone. "Is this enough proof?"

I watched as her facial expression changed from pleasant to disgusted. "Wow! This is more than proof; this will definitely get the judge's attention."

"Great, because this man is trying to destroy me and take e'erything I worked hard for. I don't want him to get a penny of my daddy's hard-earned money."

"Well, you know I'm good at what I do, and my private investigator is the best in the business. Whatever Mr. Ipswich has going on will definitely come to light. I just want you to know that sometimes divorce can get messy and things are revealed and are no longer private."

"I'm tired of this bastard controlling my life. I don't care what comes out as long as I get him out of my life. Send my assistant your invoice and whatever costs you acquire. Shawnda, I need you on this urgently."

"I assure you, your case will be top priority. I will file the divorce case in the morning on the basis of infidelity, and physical and mental abuse. And you will be hearing from me soon. Malaya, good luck on that criminal case, and please don't hesitate to call me if you need me." She got up, walked around the desk, and gave me a hug.

"Thank you so much." I left shortly after that.

I felt a slight feeling of relief when I left the lawyer's office. After all of these years of being in a fucked-up marriage, it was finally going to be over. It would've been much better if I was a widower, but I would settle for the divorce.

I got into my car and pulled off. I glanced in my rearview mirror, and I noticed that the same dark car that used to follow me was behind me. I had totally forgotten about that car. I wondered who the fuck it was, and what the hell they wanted from me. I did notice that when Trent was supposedly dead, I didn't see the car. Now that his ass was back from the dead, the car was back in the picture. I wasn't in the mood for the games. I thought about my gun that Trent took from me that day we got into it. I had no idea what happened to it, and now that I was charged with a crime, I couldn't walk into a gun store and buy one myself.

I made several turns, trying to get away from the car. I thought I did until I made a right turn, and there was the car again. Only this time, it was riding my bumper. I sped up, and the car sped up. I no longer thought this was random; I knew someone was in that car, trying to run me off the road. I was doing eighty in a thirty-five mile-per-hour zone, and the car was right on my ass. I tried my best not to cause an accident, but whoever it was behind me obviously was trying to make me do the opposite. The car sped up and rammed into me, causing me to hit the guardrail. My car stopped and shook, and my side of the car lifted up. My car started smoking.

I tried opening my car door, but it was jammed. I frantically grabbed my cell phone and dialed 911. I then crawled into the back seat and opened the back door.

Within five minutes, I heard sirens and the ambulance sound.

"Ma'am, are you okay?" a uniformed police officer ran up to me and asked.

"Yes. I'm a little shaken up, but I'm fine."

"Ma'am, what's your name, and can you tell me what happened here?"

"My name is Malaya Ipswich, and I was on my way home when I noticed a dark Charger following close behind me. I didn't think anything of it until the car sped up, and then the driver deliberately pushed me into the guardrail."

"Did you by any chance see the driver's face or get a look at the license plate?"

"The car had a dark tint, and no, I was trying to stay alive. I didn't see the license plate."

"Okay, ma'am, the ambulance is here. You might want to go with them to get yourself checked out," the young, sexy police officer said.

"Thank you, Officer, but I think I'm okay. I'm going to call AAA to get my car towed."

"Well, I'm going to make a report, ma'am." He walked off to his car.

I dialed AAA's number and waited for them to show up. The nice officer stayed out there with me until the tow truck showed up. I thanked him and got into the truck with the tow truck driver.

I spent all morning on the phone, making a claim with my insurance company. I swear, these motherfuckers love taking people's money but always give a hard time when it's time to provide service that is paid for. By the time I got off the phone with that agent , I was worn out. I was told that I could get a loaner car by this evening. That was a good thing because I needed to get around.

The girls were in school, and I was home alone as usual. I was already getting tired of being in the house all day. I decided to start going over my case. I needed to get a head start so I knew what I was up against. I walked upstairs to get my laptop and then walked into the kitchen to make a cup of tea. I stopped in the middle of the kitchen; something caught my nose, I knew that smell all too well; it was the cologne that Trent wore, Extreme Blue by Michael Kors. I spun around and walked out into the hallway. I could smell the cologne out in the hallway also, but there was no one there. I walked out to the sunroom and checked my back door. It was locked. Hmm. I was really tripping; I really needed to change these locks tomorrow because Trent had a set of keys also. I just hoped that he had enough sense not to show his face around here. The sound of the kettle whistling interrupted my thoughts. I walked back into the kitchen to make my cup of tea.

I walked into my study and cut on my computer. The first thing that I needed to do was dig deep into the charges against me, just as if I were going to defend a client. The only difference was I was my own client. I cut the radio on Pandora to kind of help settle my thoughts.

I felt a kiss on my neck! The hair on my back stood alarmed. My insides shivered as I tried to understand what the hell was going on. "Did you miss me, honey?" Trent's voice echoed through the walls of my office studio.

I quickly jumped up out of my seat and stood face to face with my soon-to-be ex-husband. "What the fuck are you doing here?"

"Malaya, this is still my home. I can come and go as I like."

"Like hell you can. You fucking set me up, and now you have the nerve to be all up in my face."

"Correction, honey, I didn't set you up. That thug you were fucking set you up. See, you were too damn smart for your own good."

"I don't have anything to say to you. Get out of my house!" I screamed. I had my cell phone in my pocket. I used my hand to search around for the button to record him. I wasn't sure if it was the right button, but there was no way to find out.

"Bitch, shut the fuck up. I told you about making a fool out of me. Do you know how embarrassed I am that my slut of a wife was running around here, fucking and sucking on these convicted felons? I knew you were a whore, but I never thought you were dumb enough to try to get me killed. Tell me, Malaya, what it is? Is his dick bigger than mine, or is it that you were just a whore who fucked and sucked any lowlife? Huh? Tell me, Malaya," he yelled. I tried to leave the room, but he blocked my path. "Answer me, bitch!" His big hand slapped across my face.

I went straight for his balls, kicking him in them. He grabbed his crotch and yelled, "Bitch, I'm going to kill you."

I was determined to get up out of there alive. I knew he was an officer, and he was experienced in killing. I ran to the kitchen and grabbed my knife, but he was one step behind me. He punched me so hard that I fell onto the counter and then ultimately to the ground. I curled up in a fetal position as he kicked and stomped me.

"I told you a long time ago, bitch, I was not the one to be fucked with. You thought you were goin' to get away with this. Huh? Where is your side nigga now? Call that boy so I can give him some of this. I should've killed your ass when I ran you off of the street the other day, but there were too many witnesses around.

His steel-toed boots made connections with my ribs. I winced as the pain became unbearable.

What was only a few minutes felt like an hour or more of torture. I held my head and starting praying to God. I knew I was going to die, but I needed to ask for forgiveness for all the wrong shit I had done in my life. "Bitch, die!" were the last words that I remembered before I passed out.

I knew I was in the hospital by the sound of beeping machines. I tried opening my eyes, but I couldn't. I used my hand to touch my face and realized that my eyes were swollen, and that was the reason why I couldn't open them. I recalled the severe beating I took from Trent. I had no idea how I got to the hospital, but I was grateful I wasn't dead. I thought I wasn't going to make it.

"Good morning, love." It was Dana.

I tried to respond, but my face was swollen. It hurt too bad to even say one word. I smiled at her.

"I'm happy to see you're awake and, don't worry, you don't have to talk. I'll do enough talking for both of us. I brought you some flowers and balloons, and Isiah sent his love. He will be up here tomorrow. Both of us can't be out of the office at the same time. Your mother came up as soon as I called her. I hope I didn't overstep my boundaries, but the girls needed somebody to take care of them."

"Thank you," I mumbled, just enough for her to hear me.

"You're in pretty bad shape. You could've died if your daughters didn't come home from school and find you lying on the ground."

"Hey, Dana, did you see my cell phone?"

"No, but I can stop by the house to get it for you."

" No, that's not necessary.."

I was hoping that my phone was still at the house, and Trent didn't pick it up. I didn't mention it to Dana. I was too embarrassed for her to listen to this man degrading me.

**

I was happy to see my mama's face. "My baby girl," she said as she rushed over to my bedside.

"Hey, Mama." The swelling on my face had gone down a little, so I was able to talk a little better.

"How you feeling?"

"Much better than a few days ago. But the doctors said my ribs were bruised, so I'm feeling real sore from all the beating."

"So, the girls are okay. They're in school, and your sisters send their love."

"Thank you for coming, Mama."

"Malaya, I know you don't feel well, but I'm very pissed off with you. Why did you get arrested, and I didn't know anything about it? I was shocked as hell when Myesha told me that the other day."

"Mama, I'm so sorry. I didn't want to get you involved in any of this."

"Involved? Child, shut your mouth, talking that nonsense. You're my child, and I need to know what's going on. I told you a long time ago to divorce his ass. That man ain't no good. He was after your money from day one. You were too blind to see that, but I saw right through him."

I couldn't say anything. Mama showed Trent respect because of me, but she always said that he wasn't right. I didn't pay her any mind back then because I was in love and thought that he was my knight in shining armor.

"Oh, here goes your cell phone. I know you need it."

"Thanks, Mama." I quickly scrolled to Voice Memo. I saw the date of the recording. It was there. "Thank you, God," I said quietly.

"So, the policeman said that it was an intruder who broke in the house and beat you up."

"Is that so? What made them think that?"

"The back door glass was broken, and the house was ransacked."

I checked the back door the day of the incident, and the glass wasn't broken. That was Trent's doing. "Mama, it wasn't an intruder; it was Trent. He came up in the house and did this to me."

"Oh, sweet Jesus. Are you sure, baby?"

"Yes, Mama, I'm sure. I have it all here on my phone."

"You need to give this to the police, so they can lock that animal up. He could've killed you."

"Mama, that man hates me for whatever reason; I don't know."

"Baby, most of these men hate women because they are jealous, and you're a threat to him. He was always inferior to you, and he knew it. His hate for you didn't start now; it just got to the boiling point."

"I'm tired, Mama, of everything. I just want this case to be over with, so I can move on with my life. I'm going to stay single for a while, so I can get myself together."

"Baby girl, you've got this, and God's got you. He won't give you more than you can bear, so give it to Him, and let go."

I smiled at her. I knew better than to get her started on that God stuff. Soon, she would be telling me I needed to get baptized. At times, I wished I had the faith that lady had because she always seemed to be so upbeat and positive even through the hardest of times.

We ended up talking for a little while longer, and then she left. I was happy that my mama was at the house with the girls because I didn't have to worry about them as much.

Six Weeks Later

Javon

The more powder I sniffed, the more I became dependent on the drug. I was spending money like water, and the money Abraham had given to me was dwindling fast. I couldn't control my appetite for the powder. I was hurting so bad that the only satisfaction I had was when I was high.

I had to figure out something fast. I couldn't go to Abraham because the nigga was on some other shit. Fuck him on the real because that nigga thought I needed him; that's why he popped up talking all that shit. He better be happy I didn't have my burner because I would've blasted his old ass for disrespecting me like that.

I was ready to bounce up out of this state. My kids were gone, so there was nothing for me anymore. Detective Pelluso kept blowing up my phone, but I wasn't in the mood to rap with this fool. I didn't know that once I decided to work with the police, it would become a fucking nuisance. I put my phone on silent to quiet down the constant ringing.

I only had eighty dollars left, and I was ready to score some more powder. I was about to walk out of the door when I heard a banging at the door. I thought it was the hotel people because today was my last day. I had no idea where I was going to get the money to pay for another month. I peeped through the peephole and quickly noticed it was Detective Pelluso and his partner. I had no idea why they were here because I told them everything I knew; plus, it wasn't time for Malaya's trial. I gritted my teeth and opened the door. "Yo, what the fuck? You can't keep popping up on me like this."

"Mr. Sanders, this is official police business. You're under arrest for the murders of Anthony Biggins and Sheila Biggins. You have the right to remain—"

"What the fuck y'all doing? Y'all do know I've got immunity."

"I'm sorry, Mr. Javon. The DA didn't accept that deal we threw you, and he issued a warrant for your arrest."

"What the fuck you mean, yo? You gave me your word! You said that if I told you everything, I would walk."

"It's not up to only me. The DA has to approve it."

"Nigga, fuck you!" I punched his ass dead in the face.

The other officer tackled me to the ground. "Stay down before I shoot your ass." He pressed his gun down in my back.

This isn't a bad idea.

I didn't stay. Instead, I used all my might and flipped his ass on his neck.

"Put your hands up! Nowwwww."

I didn't listen to them. I saw my kids' faces flash across my face. I knew then it was over for me. I lunged toward the officer and tussled him to the ground. His partner fired the first shot, which hit my chest, then the second, then the third. My foot buckled underneath me, and I fell to the ground. Blood spilled out of my mouth.

"Get some help!" the detective hollered, but it was too late. My body started shaking uncontrollably as I took one big gulp. I gasped for air. I started coughing. Tears rolled down the side of my face as everything around me turned black.

Malaya

I heard the news from Isiah that the police killed Javon this morning. I could lie and say I gave a fuck, but I won't; his ass deserved to fucking die. I was hurt that he told on me. I was more disappointed in myself that I trusted a street thug. I knew better, but my judgment was clouded because he put that dick work down. Finally, he was put out of his misery, and now I could focus on getting my life back in order.

I was finally released from the hospital. I sat waiting for Dana to pick me up. I had a new outlook on life. I was ready to start over with my life; but, before I did that, I had a few scores to settle.

"Hey, girl. Let's get out of here."

"Yes, I'm so ready." I laughed.

We walked out to the front of the hospital where she was parked. I quickly got into the car, and she pulled off. "I need you to take me to the police headquarters."

She looked at me with a long stare.

"I'm the boss. Just do what I ask you to do. Please."

"Aw, shit. She is back. The head B in charge is alive and kicking," she joked.

I smiled even though I wasn't in a joking mood. I waited for this day to come when I could finally pay these motherfuckers back. They thought Malaya Ipswich was one of these dumb bitches out here, but they had it wrong. I guessed I'd have to show them how the game was really played.

Dana parked the car, and I got out. "Do you need me to go in with you, and do you need me to call Isiah?"

"No, just stay put. Hopefully, I won't be long." I straightened my blouse, held my head high, and sashayed into the headquarters. I didn't stop to talk to the secretary. Instead, I walked directly to the DA's office. I pushed the door open and stepped inside.

"Malaya, I mean, Mrs. Ipswich, what are you doing here?"

"Hello, Devon." I took a seat.

"You know I can't talk to you without your lawyer."

"I am my own lawyer. So, let's talk, Counselor. I want to press charges against my husband, Trent Ipswich."

"Press charges? I'm lost. Help me out here."

"A month ago, I was attacked in my home, and my husband was responsible for almost killing me."

"Malaya, that is a serious allegation. Do you have any proof he did such a heinous crime?"

I reached into my purse and pulled out my phone. I hit play and put it close to him. The tape was crystal clear as Trent's voice echoed through my iPhone 6 Plus. He looked uneasy, twitching in his seat.

"That was the first matter! The second matter is I need you to drop the charges against me."

"You are fucking crazy! You know I can't do that."

"You and I both know that's a lie. You are the DA, and you call the shots."

"Malaya, I just told you I can't do that. I can offer you a plea bargain, but that's the best I can do for you."

I got up and walked to the window. I looked at the nice view that his office offered. "I wonder what Senator Muir would say if he found out that his loving son-in-law has been screwing around on his daughter. Do you think you would still be the DA?" I walked back around to the front of the desk and stared in his eyes.

"What are you trying to say, Malaya? Are you threatening me?"

"No threats, Devon. I'm a woman of my word, and I'm telling you, if you don't drop these bogus-ass charges, I will drop off a copy of this tape to the senator's office and another copy to Channel 7 Eyewitness News."

"What tape? What are you talking about?" His eyes popped opened.

I reached into my purse and pulled out my mini camcorder. I cut it on so he could watch the mini movie of himself in action.

"You bitchhhh! You recorded us?" He tried to reach for my camcorder, but I was too fast. I grabbed it and cut it off.

"I wasn't a bitch when your head was buried deep inside of my pussy or when you had your tongue deep inside of my ass. I wonder what the missus will say when she realizes her precious husband is nothing but a two-timing son of a bitch. You have exactly twenty-four hours before I go to the senator and the news. I will be waiting on that call that the charges are dropped."

"You can't fucking do this! This is blackmail. You're not going to get away with this. I will destroy you!" He stood up and pointed his finger at me, spit flying everywhere.

"You're a smart man, so I know you'll do the right thing. Twenty-four hours, Devon."

I put the camcorder and phone back into my purse. I winked at him as I walked out of the office. I got into the car.

"Is everything all right?"

"Couldn't be any better. Take me home please!"

CHAPTER THIRTEEN

Malaya

I patiently waited to get the phone call that my charges were dismissed. The anticipation was killing me, though. I knew Devon was no pushover, but I also knew that he was a man with pride, and as much as he may have wanted to go after me, I was confident that he wouldn't because of the shame he would bring down not only on his office but also on the senator and his family. It was kind of a coincidence, but this was election year, and there was no way the senator was going to risk this kind of embarrassment.

I took a glance at the time on my phone. I then looked to see if I had any missed calls. There wasn't any. I was tempted to call the DA's office but decided to give him another half hour. I cut the television on to take my mind off of the situation at hand.

"Breaking news. Yes, Ross, we're here at the police headquarters where we're waiting for District Attorney Devon Williams to step on the podium. We are the only news station present and will be bringing you a live statement in a few minutes. This is Juannita Blackmon reporting for Channel 7 Eyewitness News."

"Nooooo!" What the fuck was this nigga doing? This was not part of the fucking plan. What was the breaking news? Before I could finish that thought, the news was back from commercial.

"Today is a very somber day for my family and me. I've decided to step down from my position of being the district attorney. Anyone who knows me knows how much I love the good people of this town and love to be able to bring them justice, case after case. With that said, you must know this is not easy for me or my family, but I am going through a difficult time dealing with personal issues, and I can't serve the people the way I would love to. Please, I'm asking for privacy as my family and I deal with this personal issue. Thank you."

"Fuck you, you dirty bastard," I screamed as I threw the remote into the mirror. I grabbed my computer and Googled the state senator's office. Bingo. I called the office.

"Good afternoon. Can I speak to Senator Muir, please?"

"I'm sorry, but he's not in the office. I can transfer you to his voicemail."

"No! I need to talk to him now. I have a tape that can ruin his family and his career."

"Ma'am, what kind of tape is this?"

"Listen, lady, no disrespect, but you need to give me the senator's cell phone number, or your ass will be in the unemployment office, along with him, when this shit hits the news."

"Hold on. Here is his number."

I programmed the number into my phone, thanked the bitch, and hung up. I dialed the senator's number but got the voicemail. I knew that the minute I hung up the phone, the bitch was on the phone, calling him. My phone then rang. I looked at it; it was the senator's number.

"Hello." His thick New York accent echoed through my earpiece.

"Hello, Senator. My name is Malaya Ipswich. We've never met, but I'm sure that I have some great information that might grab your attention."

"Mrs. Ipswich, I am a very busy man, so please don't waste my time. Please get to the point."

"Okay, Senator Muir. I am about to forward a video to you." I hung up the phone.

I pulled the video up and pressed forward. Within one minute, my phone was ringing. "Mrs.

Ipswich, what kind of sick joke is this?" he asked angrily.

"I'm sorry, Senator, but this is no joke. I have a proposition for you. I have a case coming up, and I need that case to disappear in exchange for this video."

"A case? I can't get involved in no criminal case. Furthermore, I never liked the bastard. I have no idea what my daughter saw in him."

"Are you saying you don't care if the news finds out the real reason why he quit? This would make your family look bad," I tried to convince the old fool.

"Mrs. Ipswich, I will personally pay you to give it to the news stations all over the country. Maybe now my daughter will see him for what he really is."

I was shocked as hell; this man was serious. I saw that I wasn't getting anywhere with him, so I hung up. I was feeling desperate, and I was so sure that the old man would pull some strings so that this tape would not get out. But obviously, he wanted it to get out. With family like that, who really needs an enemy?

EPILOGUE

Malaya

I knew my trial date was coming up, and I was ready to take on these charges. My phone rang; it was Isiah. I picked it up to see what he wanted. "Hola, bebe. I've got some great news!"

"What are you talking about?"

"The new DA just called me and said your charges are dropped."

"You're fucking lying!"

"I'm dead ass, girly. I told you they didn't have anything on you."

"Oh, my God," I started crying out.

"What's going on down here?" Mama asked as she made her way down the stairs.

"Mama, they dropped the case against me." I dropped to my knees and started crying.

"You are one blessed woman. I told you before that you were covered by the blood of Jesus. Didn't I?"

"Yes, Mama. You sure did."

I loved how everyone was taking credit for something that I did on my own. I was the one who went after that bastard. I knew the old man talked all that shit, but he wasn't ready to take that walk.

My phone started ringing; it was the senator. "Hello, Senator. How are you doing?" I wiped my tears.

"Mrs. Ipswich, I'm sure that you're aware that the charges against you are dropped. Now, I need you to destroy that tape."

"Oh, so you don't want it to go public anymore?"

"As much as I would love to see him go under, I have to protect my daughter and my grandchild. I need to know that you're a woman of your word."

"I will destroy it. Believe it or not, I just want to be free of all charges."

"And, Mrs. Ipswich, please stay away from my son-in-law."

"Ha-ha, you have nothing to worry about. That shit between us has been dead."

"Good-bye, Mrs. Ipswich."

I hung the phone up and pumped my fist. I looked up to the ceiling. "Thank you, God!"

I was ready to start my life over. I decided to move to Maryland with Mama. The girls weren't happy, especially Myesha, but I didn't give a damn. After I found out that she was running her mouth to Trent's mother, I had to sit her ass down and let her have it. She tried to pop off, but I busted her dead in the mouth. She must've gotten the memo because, after that day, she wasn't as talkative as she used to be.

I was ready for some new scenery. I had one thing to handle before I left town, and that was to see my soon-to-be ex-husband. I drove up to the jail and walked in. I waited until my name was called, and then I walked in. I smiled at Trent, but he looked disappointed, like I wasn't the one he expected to see. "Hello, my love. How are you?"

"What the fuck do you want, Malaya?"

"I'm here to say good-bye, but I just want to know one thing. When did you start fucking boys? Were you always a faggot?"

He looked at me and smiled. I swear I wished I could slap that shit off his face.

"You know, Malaya, I've always love a tight ass and, to be honest, I tried to change, but after I married you, I realized that there's nothing a bitch can give me that these boys can't give to me."

I looked at him and shook my head. How in God's name did I not see him for the piece of shit he was?

"The girls and I are moving to Maryland—"

Before I could finish my sentence, he cut me off. "What the fuck do you mean? My fucking girls ain't going no-motherfucking-where," he yelled.

"Calm it down," a guard yelled.

"Trent, I heard you will be gone for a long time, and yes, I will be here for every court date to ensure you're given exactly what you deserve. But don't you worry; you will be someone's bitch now and get all the dick your heart desires. The divorce will be finalized soon, and your ass will get nothing. See, Trent, you should've stayed dead. I could've gotten the life insurance money. Oh, well. Too bad. I'll see you around."

"Bitch, you think you better than me 'cause you've got a few dollars? That ain't shit. I'm going to be out of here one day and, when I do, I'm coming for you, bitch! Mark my words."

"Maybe so, but until then, please enjoy your stay. I'm not scared of you; you're a weak piece of shit I should've never married. Now, go suck on one of those mean dicks and leave me the fuck alone."

"I hope you crash and die, you stupid bitch! Guards, I'm ready to go," he hollered, just like the bitch he was.

I smiled at his pitiful ass and walked away.

I got in my car and drove off!

Whew, this year had been a very crazy one, but I swear, it was a learning experience. If I had to do it all over again, I thought I would just do some things a little differently. I would've killed Trent my-damn-self, and I would've never trusted Javon's bitch ass.

"Ha-ha," I laughed out. That young nigga did have some good-ass dick, though, but not enough to get caught up in all this drama!